# CATCH ME

## JULIA CROSSWOOD

# Contents

# Prologue
## VANCE

"Mr. Newman, you seem awfully happy today."

Waiting at the bar, I wave at the bartender, ignoring the man coming to stand beside me.

"Is there a reason to celebrate?"

I cast a quick, irritable side-glance before I set my eyes back on the bartender, ordering another round for me and my crew, while the stranger remains in place.

"Can I buy you a drink to celebrate your ..."

As he waits for me to complete his sentence, I shift my attention back to him, and I demand, "Who are you?"

Taking in his slicked-down hair and his tailor-made suit while noticing the hate flickering in his eyes, I realize my question was unnecessary.

I know exactly who this man is.

"I was a nobody to you a year ago." He pauses as he leans a bit closer to me. "But, now, Mr. Newman, I'm your worst nightmare."

Grabbing the hem of his vest, I deal with his threat the way I always do.

Head-on.

"Now, now, no need to get physical." He smirks, not bothered at all with the way I'm holding him. "Besides, I wouldn't do that if I were you," he says, focusing his attention on a table in the corner where three men in suits are seated, all eyes set on me. "Wouldn't want to start a bloodbath," he continues, regarding my team, who all have had a little too much to drink.

Releasing him with a shove, I try to play this the smart way. "What the fuck is your problem?"

Another question I know the answer to. But I need to find out why he's here.

"Enrico Powell."

The answer I feared.

The name of the guy I stood face-to-face with about a year and a half ago. Who was at the wrong place at the wrong time, robbing a convenience store, drawing a gun on me, putting either him or me six feet under.

"I see I've refreshed your memory. Or shall I say, my nephew's last memory." He pauses. "My sister's only son."

And there you have it—the reason he wants to wipe me off the face of the earth.

"Get it over with," I challenge, realizing he came to get his vengeance, yet he'll never leave this room alive if he does.

"Oh no. That's not why I'm here." He chuckles. "You see, I'm a patient man. I have a lot of time on my hands. Besides, it would be too humane to end this all too quick," he says, straightening his jacket. "No, Mr. Newman. I came here today to tell you that, for the past year, I've had this personal quest to find all the people you care about, so I can return the favor. So you can experience the same pain."

As if a rope were being strapped around my throat, my chest swells with anger. "Good luck with that. There's no one."

"You're actually right." His lips spread into an evil grin. "There isn't just one person; I've actually found two."

And so the rope tightens.

Even though it's foolish to act, regardless of the backup he has, I smash my fist into his face, his head snapping back as he slightly stumbles backward. His men are by his side in the blink of an eye. If it wasn't for him signaling for them to stay put, they would have me by the throat.

"Is there a problem here?" Brad—my friend and partner—asks, materializing beside me, his hand on my chest because he knows I never throw just one punch.

"No problem here. We're done," the man answers as he takes out a handkerchief, casually wiping away the droplets of blood from his nose. "Have a good night, Mr. Newman," he says right before he turns around and leaves the bar with his men in tow.

"Is that ..."

"Frank Calvetti," I finish Brad's question.

My personal horror story.

"We need to go," I bark at him as I slide my hand into my pocket, refraining myself from calling Matthew right this second. Instead, I squeeze my phone hard while I digest the fact that my assumption about the Mafia wanting revenge has just been confirmed.

I'm not a religious man, yet I feel a sudden need to pray, hoping they're not about to make my biggest fear come true.

# Chapter 1
## LAUREN

"I'm getting you out of here."

Standing in front of the Delta Tau Delta mansion, its facade illuminated by red and green neon lights, I grab ahold of my sister's arm, ready to drag her away from this place.

"Come on, Lauren," Kate pleads, pulling back while she fixes her hazel eyes on me, clueless as to what she's begging for. "We're here now. Besides, we can't ditch Amy and Olivia," she continues.

She has a point. I should have stopped this insanity before I drove us here.

"I'll be fine," she says while giving my hand a gentle squeeze.

"Fine, but you need to—"

"Stick with the group? Refuse drinks from others? Don't worry, sis; I'm twenty years old. I can handle myself."

Looking her up and down—her long, dark hair twisted up into a loose bun, her five-foot-four body curved in a subtle way—I notice how she's grown into a beautiful young woman. Something I rarely see. The fact of her health being a constant issue throughout our tough childhood clouds what's right in front of me.

"You'll always be my little sister."

"Little?" She snorts. "Are we back to that? One inch." She pauses, raising the palm of her hand to stop me from

4

interrupting. "Or that you left the womb forty minutes earlier? I bet, if nature had decided differently, you'd still be the overprotective sister."

*Absolutely.*

"But I did go first. So, I'm going to baby you until you're old and gray."

*I have to.*

We grew up without a father and with a drunk-driving mother who crashed her car into a tree when we were ten, so she's the only family I have left.

"You don't have to do this for me," I assure her, knowing how she tends to feel obligated to go out with me every once in a while.

"I'm not." She shakes her head. "I just want the full college experience," she continues as she blinks one too many times, confirming that she's hiding the real reason she's here.

"Ladies, let's get this party started!" Amy shouts, her body filling up the small space between Kate and me before her arm hooks around my neck.

Amy is my partner in crime when I hit a party. But, when my sister tags along, I'm just a bundle of stress.

"We were just about to go home," I state as I slide off Amy's arm.

"No way! We dressed up for this!" Amy complains.

My eyebrows shoot up to the night sky as I take in the matching clothes we bought just yesterday. Since it's a sports theme, we got Dodgers jerseys. Kate and I matched it with tight jeans while Amy spiced it up by wearing a short red skirt that'll just draw in all the douche bags.

*Great.*

"Let's just go and see how it is. If it's bad, we'll go home," Kate says in that angelic voice of hers.

I sigh, realizing I lost this battle the moment Kate decided to add a frat party to her bucket list for whatever reason she has in her mind.

"Perfect," Amy squeaks, clapping her hands before she herds us into the waiting line of this madhouse.

*Oh boy.*

One hour later, and I'm slowly thawing from the heat of the party, completely accustomed to the smell of beer and sweat.

Even though the football team seems to dominate the dance floor, wearing their shoulder pads and giant helmets, Amy and I have managed to find a spot where we actually have space to breathe and do a few hip swings, if we're lucky.

But I don't mind. I'm too busy keeping my eyes focused on a nearby couch where Kate and her friend Olivia have settled to watch a beer pong contest. I know it's their way of enjoying a party, lying back with a soda in hand. And yet, it still hurts to see my sister stuck on a couch when she could be dancing beside me.

Ever since the death of our mother, she quit her dancing classes, unable to practice or perform without our mom— her biggest fan—by her side. Then again, this wouldn't be the right place for her to show her moves, based on the type of guys surrounding us. And I know Amy has got something to do with it.

Is it the way she moves her body to the beat of the music while her eyes are dancing across the room? Or her lush blonde hair and round curves, which make her stand out in this crowd?

I have no clue.

But, once more, she's gathered a male crowd, one who isn't only interested in her.

A brush of a hand just above my hip is my first warning.

*I can live with that.*

A knee between my legs, my second.

*Now, that's more of a problem.*

Turning around, I face the guy who's invading my personal bubble.

He's got perfect white teeth, way too much gel in his hair, and somewhat of a baby face. Placing both hands on his basketball shirt, I'm about to push him away when someone in the crowd captures my attention.

*He's* here.

In the midst of all these students dancing and drinking, I see him leaning against the wall as he lifts a red Solo cup to his mouth, all the while intently watching me.

How I hate this new reflex I've adapted.

And yet, I can't stop myself from sweeping in all his features, as if it were the very first time I'd laid eyes on him.

His broad shoulders, hidden beneath a dark hoodie. His strong, chiseled jawline, the only part that's never concealed by his burgundy baseball cap.

But, most of all, his captivating, dark eyes, which tend to meet mine every so often. And, when they do, I end up fighting this urge that wants to erase all my values about the male species. Or forget the fact that he has the tendencies of a stalker—shopping at Walmart when I'm getting my groceries, eating at the same restaurant where I'm having lunch, showing up at every party I'm at.

Like a shadow, he's always around, stirring up certain emotions I'd rather ignore.

If it wasn't for Mason Scott—my stalker's best friend and the handsome blue-eyed guy who shares a few classes with Kate and me—assuring me that *he's* harmless, I would've called the cops.

But, now, I'm left with two impossible choices.

Confront him.

*No way. If the guy doesn't have the nerve to approach me, I won't either.*

Or feign ignorance.

*Yeah, still working on that one.*

Basically, I'm stuck, haunted by what's probably a six-foot-two body that tends to disrupt my life on a daily basis. Like, now, when all my zoning out has given Mr. Baby Face the opportunity to move to second base, his hands beneath my loosely hanging jersey, his fingers fiddling with the waistband of my jeans.

I'm perfectly aware, but somehow, I'm more intrigued by *his* reaction and *his* persistent glare, which hasn't relented these past few minutes.

*Is it something I did? Or maybe my stranger's roaming hands are bothering him?*

And, while Mr. Baby Face slides his hand up my spine and toward my bra, I bite my lip, refraining myself from lifting my knee just yet. My eyes are still set on *him* as I wait for him to make his move.

Plastered to the wall, he remains in place.

All my patience is in vain.

I'm about to give Mr. Roaming Hands a painful message when I finally see *him* pushing himself off the wall.

My heart pumps faster than the beat of the music.

My breath is caught in my throat as I wait for him to move closer. He still has a distance to cover.

But then I see him shift his gaze to Mason, who's standing nearby, *his* lips moving for a good ten seconds before he turns around and walks away without another look, leaving me with my heart slamming against my chest while Mason's eyes zone in on me.

*That's it.*

I push Mr. Grabby Hands off of me.

Stumbling back a step, he throws his hands in the air. "What's your problem?"

"You," I snap, hoping he'll get the message.

He's part of the reason I got distracted from what really matters. Shifting my gaze back to the couch, I notice how Kate and Olivia have been replaced with three drunken cheerleaders.

Turning toward Amy, who's dancing with a guy right next to me, I ask, "Where are they?"

"Relax. They went to the restroom."

I can't.

Not when she's wandering around in a frat house full of drunk people.

"Be right back!" I'm about to worm my way through when Amy's clammy hand stops me from leaving.

Leaning in closer, she shouts, "Don't go. I told them we'd be here. We'll lose each other."

I'd rather ignore her suggestion, but I know she's right. Even a phone call seems impossible with the music blaring this loud. And yet, standing around feels so wrong.

"I need a drink." I point to the punch bowl on a nearby table before I make my way over and pour myself a cup.

"Was that Liam again?" Amy asks as she joins me while I'm downing my second cup with big gulps, welcoming the burning sensation down my throat.

Shaking my head, I try to avoid the forbidden topic. She should know better than to talk about *him*, much less use *his* name.

Ignorance is bliss—or it should be. But, for some reason, it's not working.

Refilling my cup, I keep my eyes on the bowl when, all of a sudden, the fire alarm starts blaring through the house. The deafening sound sobers up an entire crowd in the blink of an eye, including me.

My thoughts go out to one person.

*Kate.*

My cup splashes to the ground as I dig into my pocket, removing my phone, while Amy grabs my arm, urging me to follow the throng of people toward the exit.

"We need to leave!"

By now, the music has been shut down. Bright lights illuminate the room as everyone starts pushing their way out. With Amy's hand still wrapped around my arm, I let her pull me along as I put my phone to my ear, calling Kate numerous times without an answer, as each call finishes with her voice mail.

*No. No. No.*

Looking down at my screen, I focus on the picture I've linked to my sister's phone number. Kate and me at Malibu beach, wearing identical red sunglasses, broad smiles plastered on our faces.

Some people say twins have this special connection, this unique link. I've never believed it to be true. But, today, I really hope it's not.

Because my insides are screaming.

My legs tremble with every step I take.

And then there's the confirmation.

A gun goes off.

One shot.

A sound that triggers everyone to move even faster as chaos erupts around us. The hands on my back push harder, forcing me to move forward at a quick pace, one I'd better follow if I don't want to end up being trampled to death.

Amy keeps a solid hold on my arm as we make it out of the living room and into the hallway.

Everybody's pushing toward the back, not using the exit in the front. They all want to leave, except for me.

I can't.

"Lauren," Amy pleads, feeling my hesitation.

"Go see if they're outside!" I yell, slipping out of her hold, as she's being pushed toward the back door.

Instead, I turn around and make my way through the crowd while every face I cross displays one thing.

*Fear.*

We're all fueled by it. Only I don't fear for my own life. I've always been reckless with it. It's the fear of losing the only family member I have left. She could be somewhere in this house, scared or hurt. I'm not leaving until I'm a hundred percent sure she's not here.

The more I move in the opposite way, the fewer people I have to fight to make my way over, and still, I haven't found Kate.

"Where is the restroom?" I demand as I stop a guy from moving past me.

He shies away from my touch, but I block his path with my body.

"Where is it?"

I've picked a guy about my height; otherwise, he probably would've walked right over me. My five feet five inches aren't that imposing.

"In the back and upstairs," he stammers.

My eyes shift to the stairs at the end of the hallway.

And, even though he's making his way around me, he warns me, "But I wouldn't go there if I were you. The shooter was—"

Say no more.

I rush past him, about to reach the stairs, when someone's scream halts me in my tracks, "Lauren, stop!"

Looking over my shoulder, I see Mason is taking a similar path through the crowd, eyes set on me. I know exactly what he's trying to do. The guy's a charmer. Sweeping women off their feet or rescuing them from Paul, the campus douche bag, is something he does on a daily basis. Ever since he's been keeping Paul away from Kate, I've added him to my very short decent-guy list.

Even so, he's still friends with *him*, which makes Mason someone I try to avoid as much as possible. Besides, I'm used to doing things on my own.

Waving him off, I let him know I'm fine before I turn around and take the stairs two steps at a time before a deserted corridor comes into view.

About to make a turn to the left, I notice how the floor on my right side is stained with dark droplets, a trail running all the way into a room.

A rush of adrenaline floods my veins, urging me to get the confirmation that my gut feeling is wrong, that my sister isn't lying on the floor, bleeding out in someone's room.

As if wading through a swamp of quicksand, I reach the door, and reality slams me in the chest.

*Kate.*

Her stomach is covered in blood, and *he*, of all people, is on his knees beside her, his hands pressing down on the bloodied spot.

My hand braces the doorframe, my fingers digging into the molding, while my body convulses with emotion.

Only the voice of my sister gets me out of my comatose state.

"Lauren?"

Only she can bring out my strongest and weakest sides.

"I'm here," I rasp.

I take one step forward but then one step back, my back crashing into someone's chest. I notice the arm that's curved around my waist.

Looking up, I see Mason standing behind me, beholding the horror in front of us. With his grip loosening, I tear away from him, rushing toward my sister.

I fall to my knees beside her, my hands shaking, as I'm unsure of what to do with them. "What happened?"

"You came." She smiles.

But her smile never reaches her eyes.

"Where else would I be?" I croak, fighting back my tears as I take ahold of her hand, my finger flicking over the word *sisters* engraved on top of her silver bracelet, identical to mine.

We bought them together for our eighteenth birthday. It's the only jewelry I always wear.

Holding her hand, I demand, "Who did this?"

"There was a guy. He wanted me to go with him." She squeezes her eyes closed before she continues, "I'm so sorry, Lauren. I tried my best to get away, but he—"

A hiss of pain escapes her mouth before she tries to continue.

I shush her, refraining from asking more questions since she's already extremely pale.

Tucking my hair behind my ear, I lean my forehead against hers, something I did a lot when we were little. When she woke up from a nightmare, I would do the exact same thing to calm her down.

"Don't be sorry. You did great," I assure her.

And, while there's a lot of commotion around us, I keep my focus on Kate, on her breathing.

Until it starts to falter.

Until her hazel eyes no longer look into mine.

Until my own breath starts to sputter.

A jerk on my arm.

People yelling.

Bits and pieces of rescue scenes from television invading my consciousness.

*Stop the bleeding. Pressure on the wound. What the hell have I been doing?*

I reach out to her stomach, my hands covering up every spot that's stained in blood, while I try to push away *his* hands. He's clearly not doing this the right way.

*Stop the bleeding, Lauren. Save her.*

I give his hands another shove to get my hands on the wound.

*You're her big sister. Not him.*

I push harder.

Until his voice orders me to leave, and Mason's hand grabs my shoulder.

*I can't leave. Kate needs me. We're aligned now. I've felt it. She can't leave me, not now.*

Grabbing ahold of her hand, I squeeze it hard. "Don't you dare leave me! Don't you dare!" I shout, but the whole thing comes out as one big sob.

Incomprehensible.

It doesn't matter.

Only Kate needs to understand.

Only she needs to know that there is no way she can leave me behind.

But there's no sign of life.

My sister is still unmovable on the floor while two EMTs rush into the room.

Too much blood.

Too many hands on my sister's lifeless body.

Mason is pulling me up and away from my sister.

Away from *him*.

*He's* still pressing down on Kate's stomach when he looks up, fixing eyes on the person behind me, yelling something.

But I'm beyond hearing.

There's only a ringing silence.

An arm crossed over my chest.

*Mason.*

He's trying to get me away from Kate.

*She's all I have left.*

Pushing my full body weight in the opposite direction, I try to free myself from his grasp.

Where there was gentleness before, now, it's gone. The more I struggle, the harder he tugs back, squeezing all the air out of my lungs.

Mason's determination trumps my despair.

I beg him to leave me be. And, when that doesn't work, I scream every curse word that comes to mind. But my wishes are ignored while he drags me down the stairs and out the back door.

The last image I have of my sister is one of her unconscious as she's bleeding out.

My bones turn to mush.

My body is empty and limp as a rag doll.

Holding me across the chest, Mason now puts an arm around my back and under my legs, cradling me to his chest.

I'm beyond caring.

All I can see is Kate lying there.

Her blood everywhere.

It's sickening.

My stomach rolls with nausea.

Mason manages to get me on my feet right before the vomit reaches my mouth and I cover his right shoe with it.

"Shit," he curses, one arm around my waist while the other arm is holding my hair back.

I should apologize. I should feel guilty, embarrassed. But I'm empty.

As much as I want to be left alone, to fall apart without an audience, Mason won't let me.

Once I'm done emptying my stomach, he snakes an arm around my middle before he pulls my left arm around his neck, supporting me as much as possible while we walk further away from the house, across the mansion's backyard, and through an alley toward another street.

"I can't," I croak, the queasiness now conquering my whole body as my legs threaten to give out once more.

"Where is that fucking car?" Mason yells right before my vision blurs, and I slip into unconsciousness.

# CHAPTER 2
## MASON

"Where is that fucking car?" I yell while I catch Lauren right before she face-plants onto the pavement.

Holding her up with one arm, I check my phone. There's one text with Jaden's location, which is different from what we agreed.

*Fucking perimeter.*

The police are keeping him away from the crime scene.

Cradling Lauren's body close to my chest, I check my surroundings once again before I cross the street and run into someone's yard.

Police sirens wail in the distance as I take a longer route toward the awaiting car. Anything to avoid running into an officer and ending up in a police station for the rest of the night.

Luckily, there's no one in sight, the street practically deserted. A small relief for my anxious mind while my body's high on adrenaline.

*I need to get her out of here.*

Squeezing her body closer to mine, I run one more block before I see a gray Volvo parked at the curb.

I slide into the backseat, settling Lauren in my lap.

"What's wrong with her?" Jaden prods the moment he notices Lauren's unconscious state.

Raising my hand, I assure him, "She's fine," stating a fact when it's more of an uncertainty.

Still, I want him to remain behind the wheel. I didn't just ditch Liam and run two blocks with Lauren passed out in my arms to sit here and chitchat while we're still out in the open.

"Just get us out of here," I urge as I take a glance out the window.

And, while Jaden takes off, I look down at Lauren, my hand encircling her wrist, her heart still pumping a solid beat.

Shifting a little more behind Jaden's seat, I set aside the guilt for what I'm about to do. Still, there's no way in hell I'll sit here and assume she's fine. And, since her hands and shirt are covered with stains of blood, I need to confirm that she wasn't harmed before I got to her.

Peeling her bloodstained jersey upward with one hand, illuminating her stomach and upper chest with my phone in my other hand, I skid my fingertips over her unscathed stomach to confirm that she isn't hurt.

Physically, she's fine.

Emotionally, a whole other story.

I'm good with the ladies. I feel them. But, tonight, I'd rather smash some faces instead of comfort a girl who has every right to lose her shit.

If it wasn't for the task at hand, I would lose it myself.

# Chapter 3
## LIAM

*Eight Months Ago*

"Who is it?" I take another swig of my beer as I scan the crowd. "Is it the blonde girl?"

"What are you talking about?" Mason's eyes flicker briefly in my direction before returning to the dance floor.

"I'm talking about you moving all the way from east to west, interrupting your father's SPISe training program, abandoning your best friend"—I point a thumb at my chest—"who had to finish it on his own. And I didn't even get a reasonable explanation."

"I told you, I was visiting family."

"Mase, dude, I've got an associate's degree in law enforcement, just like you. Although I'm starting to doubt how you earned yours." Mason flails his hand toward my head, which I avert nicely, before I continue, "Just admit that you've already been assigned by your brother. And, now, Matthew is trying to get me on it, too."

"You need a vacation."

"Exactly," I say, followed by an irritated sigh. "Not a job."

He grabs his soda and motions for me to follow him as he moves closer to the dancing crowd. I follow his gaze to a certain spot, which is not the blonde girl but the one dancing next to her. She's short, as in doesn't-even-reach-my-chin short. Her long, dark hair hangs loosely down her back, and she's wearing a tank top and tight jeans that show off her slim figure.

"The brunette?"

"I'm in over my head," he confesses, trailing a hand through his hair. "And, since it's a delicate case, you are the perfect candidate."

*Fuck.*

My sister's problems are finally being dealt with. I'm not ready to add more female drama to my life right now.

"Matthew has a nasty way of asking." I deflect the issue while I keep my eyes on her—how she's swaying her hips in sync with the beat of the music, how she's got her hands in the air while her eyes are closed.

"I know. He was afraid you would say no."

An unfounded fear.

If it were anyone else, I would've left already. But I can't say no to the Scott brothers. They've helped me a lot this past year, monitoring my sister so that I wouldn't find her dead body in a gutter because she overdosed on drugs. They used to be friends, but now, I consider them family.

So, I finish my drink and ask the one question that'll probably pull me in completely, "What's her story?"

"You mean, what's *their* story?"

When I shake my head in confusion, he nods his head toward another girl sitting at a table, hugging her knees to her chest as she's talking to someone next to her.

"Twins. I've been keeping an eye out on the both of them. But it's getting harder by the day."

I look back at the girl who's got the guy in front of her wrapped around her body now. "Her boyfriend will look out for her."

"That's not her boyfriend," Mason scoffs.

"What?"

"She doesn't do boyfriends."

I glare at the guy who's got his hands all over her while I suppress the sudden urge to waltz through the crowd and rip him off her. Something I've done too many times for my younger sister who loved to mess around, playing a dangerous game with guys who were too wasted to know when to stop.

"Then, what the hell is she doing?"

"What can I say?" He sighs. "I'm in *way* over my head."

*Fuck.*

"I can't do this again." I shake my head, turning around, as I'm about to take a restroom break to clear my head.

"Look," Mason says, grabbing hold of my arm, mistaking my retreat for refusal, "I get it. You just got Catherine into rehab." He sighs again. "I would never ask if it wasn't absolutely necessary," he continues, all playfulness gone. "Just help me out until we find someone who's capable and trustworthy enough to handle this case."

I have no clue what this case is about or how these girls ended up needing Scotts' Private Investigation and Security services, but when Mason gets all serious, I know they're in deep.

"I'll do it, but I'm keeping an eye on her." I motion with my head to the brunette sipping a Coke, the epitome of good.

"Kate."

"Huh?"

"Her name is Kate. I'll take Lauren."

*Lauren.*

I turn my head back toward her, unable to stop myself from giving her another glance to check if she's still there and not being dragged outside. She'll never be able to stop the guy with that fragile, short body of hers.

"Thanks, bro." Mason puts a hand on my shoulder. "Good to have you here."

Tearing my eyes away from Lauren, I remind myself that I have to keep an eye on Kate, who's still in the exact same spot. "You need another soda?"

"Yes," he clips, eyes on the dance floor.

Walking toward the bar, I now understand Mason's desperate cry for help. Somehow, I get the feeling that even the two of us won't be enough.

For *Lauren.*

# CHAPTER 4
## LAUREN



*Present*

Unconsciousness, a void without any pain, hidden from reality.

Coming out of it, I still feel numb.

Until I smell the scent of a man's cologne.

Until I feel how my head is tucked against the crook of someone's neck.

Until I notice I'm in Mason's arms.

Then, I remember everything.

The flashes of tonight's nightmare flood my mind as my stomach tightens in knots. Afraid that I'll cover myself in vomit once more, I slap a hand over my mouth.

"Hold on," Mason whispers as he picks up speed, sprinting through a narrow hallway and into a white-tiled bathroom where he sets my feet on the floor right in front of the toilet.

Sinking down onto my knees, I grab ahold of the seat, throwing up the little contents left in my stomach, while Mason's hands pull back the strands of hair that threaten to spill into the toilet.

I retch and vomit until there's nothing left. Then, I pull back, sliding my butt over the bathroom floor until my back hits a cold wall.

If only I could get rid of this horrible truth as easily as the food in my stomach. But I can't, and even though I rarely shed a tear, I cry uncontrollably, my body shaking with every tortured sob that escapes my mouth, as I rest my head on my raised knees to lock Mason out. But, when I feel a brush of something on my left side, followed by his arm snaking around my neck, drawing my body closer to the warmth of his, I know he won't leave me alone.

With no energy left to resist, I let him hold me while I fall apart.


"Let's get you to bed," a soft voice says right before I feel the closeness of someone's body, an arm sliding around my back and another under my knees.

Opening my eyes, I become aware of my surroundings, of Mason, who's trying to lift me off the bathroom floor.

I scramble away from him, my eyes set on his Converse sneakers glued to the floor, waiting for them to move closer. Instead, they leave, and I'm finally alone.

Tilting my head backward, I lift up my shoulders to get rid of the stiffness in my neck before my gaze settles on my fingers covered in dried blood.

Another reminder.

Grabbing a scrub sponge from the edge of the bathtub, I have only one thing in mind; I want it gone.

No. More. Stains.

"Stop!" Mason yells, slapping the sponge out of my hands. "They're clean," he snaps, seizing my wrists as he shakes my hands.

My eyes focused on my red-blotched fingers, I notice now how I've successfully removed every drop of my sister's blood. Yet, somehow, it feels worse, as if I just tried to erase her.

"Let's get you in some clean clothes," he says, releasing my hands. "I'll help you."

I haven't said a word, hoping he'd go, but now, I realize he needs to hear me say it.

"Don't." I lift up my head before I continue, "Just leave me be."

A full sentence, a clear message.

"I'm not leaving, Lauren. Now, lift your arms," he commands, reaching out for the hem of my jersey.

I've been too compliant and tolerated a lot of his behavior, and while I was busy falling apart, I even let him tear me away from my sister.

Now is the time to fight back, for Kate, as I refuse to believe she isn't somewhere, doing the exact same thing.

Connecting with his piercing blue eyes, I power up my stubbornness and determination—two characteristics that have gotten me through hard times in the past—and I take away the only reason for keeping me here. "I'm fine."

Mason's earnest yet unwavering look is enough for me to realize that my words alone will never suffice.

Eyes set on the door, I try to maneuver around him when an arm wraps around my waist.

"I can't let you leave."

My eyes widen with disbelief as I stare up at him, noticing the apologetic look on his face.

*Why is he doing this?*

I can't even comprehend how I ended up here in the first place, let alone the role he's taking. Still, I wouldn't be Lauren Miller if I didn't make another attempt to leave, which ends up with him lifting me up and putting me back where I initially was.

Without a word, he motions to a gray shirt and a pair of sweatpants on the side of the bath.

I want to refuse, but considering the strength he just displayed, how he's towering above me, it's enough for me to stop my physical fight.

*I'll have to find another way.*

Grabbing the shirt and putting it over mine, I notice how Mason follows my every move, opening and closing his mouth, clearly mulling over the fact that I didn't get rid of my stained shirt.

*I can't.*

I still feel awful for rubbing my hands like a madman, getting her blood off as if it were a disease.

Once I'm finished, he takes my hand and pulls me along through the hallway and into a bedroom.

"You can sleep in my bed. I'll sleep on the floor." He motions toward a mattress lying next to the bed. "If you need anything, I'll be here."

Another vow.

I look up at him, his defensive stance signaling that he'll fight me on this, too. So, I turn around and get into bed with my sneakers still attached to my feet, crawling beneath the dark covers smelling of him.

Closing my eyes, I hear him turn off the lights and settle on the mattress beside me. After I hear no more tussling, his breath as regular as someone who's fast asleep, I open my eyes to see Mason's blue ones staring right back at me.

"Sleep," he commands.

And, while I try a few more times to fake sleep, stretching my patience to a maximum, I actually drift off.

# Chapter 5
## LAUREN

Going in and out of sleep all night, I open my eyes to notice the unoccupied mattress on the floor.

I take another quick scan of the room until I'm sure.

*He's finally gone.*

In seconds, I'm out of bed, losing Mason's shirt before I slide into an oversize black hoodie that was draped over a chair. Tapping my pocket one more time to check if my phone is still in place, I make my way out the door, taking a much-needed bathroom break. Then, I slowly tiptoe down the stairs while I listen in on the heated discussion going on in the living room.

Several male voices.

All of them unfamiliar.

I walk up to the front door and wrap my hand around the door handle when I hear Greg's voice, my adoptive father.

*He's here?*

"Thinking that won't help us. He'll handle it," someone says in a steady, resolute voice. "We have to make a decision about Lauren," he continues.

I hold my breath at the sound of my name.

There's silence before I hear Greg's gruff voice again. "She can't stay with me any longer."

My heart stops mid-beat, and I almost cough to get another breath. Instead, I inhale through my nose and out through my mouth while I swallow away the lump that almost betrayed me. I don't even know why I would react to something I always knew would happen.

"We'll take her with us to New York," someone says, overconfident.

*Another wannabe parent? No, it ends here. I'm almost twenty-one. I'll manage on my own.*

I push down the handle to realize the door is locked, no key.

*I have to get out of here.*

Turning around, I take the only option that's left without them noticing, which is up the stairs.

Running from one room to another, I check every window to see which one has the easiest and safest way down. Turns out, the master bedroom has a lower-level roof.

My best way out.

I take another glimpse in the direction of the hallway when I notice a set of car keys on the nightstand. It would make my getaway a lot faster, and I definitely need to buy myself enough time to get away from them. And Greg. It wouldn't be the first time he used his detective skills to get his way.

I snatch the keys off the nightstand, and then I get my butt out the window and down the drainpipe.

Once I'm safely on the ground, I press the unlock button, and the headlights of a red Dodge Charger parked a little further down the road lights up.

I jog to the driver's side and slide behind the wheel. There's no silent way to start a car, so I hold my breath as I turn the key, maneuvering the car smoothly away from the house and out onto the street.

Driving has always given me a sense of freedom, a feeling of being in control. But, today, it's bittersweet.

Greg bought everything we needed, made home-cooked meals, gave us both a shot at a good college education. Regardless of that, I couldn't hug him and never gave him any gratitude for the efforts he made. My wall thick and high enough to keep him at a distance.

But, now, I realize he somehow managed to crawl over without my knowing.

For that ignorance, I'm paying the price.

Because of that blindness, I'm sitting here, behind the wheel, tears welling in my eyes, as I've learned another hard lesson.

*No one can be trusted.*

Driving north, I've been sticking to deserted roads to avoid running into one of Greg's colleagues. My first priority is to cover some distance before I get rid of this car and take some time to find out at which hospital they're keeping Kate. I'll just have to hitchhike or use public transportation to get there.

Until then, I'm surrounded by nothingness, apart from a fast-approaching car behind me. I'm already above the speed limit, but this guy seems to be in a hurry since he's rapidly closing in on me.

Afraid that they're catching me before I have the time to find Kate, I put the pedal to the metal to get away from my pursuer.

Trying and failing.

The massive truck clearly has more muscle power, as the distance in between our cars is shrinking rapidly. I can't outrun him. And, if it's Greg, I already lost the second he saw me. He can be as persistent as I'm stubborn.

I ease up on the gas while I shift my gaze to the left, waiting for him to pass me. Only there's no one there. Fixing my eyes back on the rearview mirror, I get to witness when the truck crashes into my bumper, my body jolting from the impact.

*Oh. My. God. Greg wouldn't. Would he?*

I don't have a lot of time to dwell on that thought, too busy keeping my car under control while I reach out for my seat belt—something I tend to forget, but somehow, I believe it can serve its purpose now.

Once my seat belt clicks into place, I glare over my shoulder. All I can see is the sky reflecting off the windshield, which is masking the driver, who is about to do it again. And, since this car isn't faster than his, the only thing I can do is brace for impact. This time, he hits me even harder, and my car starts to swerve to the right.

I try to counter the movement and regain control, but when he hits me one more time, I completely lose it. My hands holding the steering wheel in a firm grip, I brace myself. My car is getting pushed off the road, and since there's a ditch alongside the road, my car starts to roll.

Game over.

# CHAPTER 6
## LIAM

I slam my hand on the steering wheel as I gun the engine.

"We'll find her," Mason assures me.

He's in the passenger seat, reining in his anger, too busy keeping me calm since I'm the one driving one hundred miles per hour.

Ironic really—how I'm generally the composed one.

Only, when it comes to her, I *always* lose control.

After everything that happened, after all we did, she still decided to climb out of a window and steal Mason's car to run away. Another reminder that she's capable of only making fucked up decisions. As if this whole situation isn't already unbearable.

Squeezing the wheel, I fight the urge to spin my car around and drive away, mirroring her actions. Yet I'm no quitter. I'll get her ass back where it belongs, and then Jaden can take over, so Lauren Miller will no longer be my problem to solve.

"We're almost there," Mason informs, eyeing the cell phone in his hand, which displays a map with Lauren's exact location.

She did do something right—taking her phone with her. She's clueless that we've been tracking her for a while now. We installed an app on her phone, a necessity to follow her around. But, now, it brings us to a deserted road, not a building in sight, only a glimpse of something red, which isn't even on the road.

My gut screams in agony while I stomp harder on the gas until I see that this red blur is in fact Mason's car upside down, lying about forty feet off the road.

"Shit!" Mason yells.

It's more like hell.

It hasn't even been a day.

Merely twelve hours ago.

When I had Kate in my arms.

When I felt it for the very first time.

A fear that choked the life out of me.

And, now, it is threatening to overwhelm me again.

"Ambulance," I croak before I drive the car off the road and into the dirt.

The ditch gives us a few jostles, but it's nothing this car can't handle.

Not that it matters.

Because I would drive any car into this ditch right now.

"We've got an unconscious girl trapped in a car," Mason rambles. He gives the operator further details.

I screech to a halt behind the red Dodge Charger before I scramble out of the car with only one thing on my mind.

*She has to be fine.*

*She has to be alive.*

I sprint to the driver's door, sliding the last few feet on my knees.

No training could have prepared me for this.

No drill could have decelerated my heart rate.

Through the shattered window, I see how Lauren is hanging upside down with closed eyes. Her seat belt is holding her in place while her arms hang lifelessly downward, and her dark brown hair is sprawled out onto the ceiling of the car.

We've never touched.

Not intentionally.

Wrapping my hand around her wrist to feel a solid heartbeat thumping against my fingers is not what I had in mind for how our first physical contact was going to be.

"Is she—" Mason chokes, unable to complete his sentence as he kneels beside me, his phone to his ear.

"She's got a pulse," I confirm. "We need to get her out."

I'm not waiting for Mason to end his call, and I definitely won't leave her like this until the ambulance arrives. A wrecked car is a ticking time bomb.

"What do you need me to do?" Mason demands once he's finished his phone call, and I've cracked open the door.

"I'll hold her in place while you undo her seat belt."

He jumps up and squeezes my shoulder. "I'll try to get in on the other side," he says before he moves to the passenger side.

Once I've placed my shoulder in the crook of her body, my left arm crossed over her lap and my right arm behind her back, I wait for Mason to unbuckle her seat belt.

"It's jammed."

"Fuck!" I'm losing my goddamn mind, if I haven't already lost it.

"I've got a pocketknife," Mason suggests.

At least one of us is able to think rationally. I can't. Not with her hanging upside down. When every second is one too many.

"Hold her up," he demands before he cuts the seat belt and rips it out of the way.

While I hold and support her head and neck, Mason takes her legs. Once we've got her in a horizontal position, I lower her onto my lap and lift her up to my chest, her head in the crook of my neck while my right arm secures her upper body in place.

Afraid that I'll damage her spine or neck by making a wrong move, I keep her in this position while I slowly crawl backward out of the Dodge Charger's cramped interior until there's a safe distance between us and the car.

"Her head." Mason's hand reaches out to touch her hair. "She's bleeding."

I shift my gaze to the spot he's looking at, and I notice a gaping wound along her right temple.

Mason runs off to the car to get the emergency kit. When he's back, he places a sterile compress against the wound.

"Keep pressure on it," he commands as he waits for me to take over. "I'll check her out."

Mason is still the composed one, which is a rarity.

But the balance has shifted. With me being out of control, he just had to take the opposite side.

While he's busy looking for other wounds, I keep my eyes focused on the rise and fall of her chest until the ambulance arrives, and two EMTs rush to her side to check her vitals.

"We need to move her," the youngest EMT explains when they've finished their brief examination. "We're losing valuable time."

As hard as it is to let go of her, I let the EMT click a neck brace into place before they carefully lift her up onto a stretcher.

I hover close around her gurney, and when they slide her into the back of the ambulance, I get in beside her.

*Screw family policy. I'm not leaving her.*

It doesn't take a word for the EMTs to know I'll be joining them or for Mason to know that he'll be driving solo to the hospital.


Arriving at the hospital, they swiftly cart her off while I'm forced to stay behind. One of the nurses makes sure of that.

"Let them take care of her," she advises, a hand to my chest.

And I'm forced to let Lauren go.

Forced to let them do their job because I've failed mine.

Again.

It hits me in the face, and all I want is to hit back. So, I do, slamming my fist against the nearest wall.

I welcome the physical pain because the emotional pain is unbearable. My veins fill with adrenaline that rips through my body, daring me to retaliate, urging me to pick up a nearby chair and fling it against the wall.

Three chairs.

That's how long it takes before someone grabs hold of me and stops this insanity by restraining my upper body from behind.

I'm about to make a countermove when I hear, "Liam!" shouted from across the hall.

Mason's here—my sanity for the day.

"Let him go," he says, coming to my side. "He'll be okay."

*I won't.*

Today's and yesterday's events will haunt me for the rest of my life regardless of the outcome. No amount of chairs will change that.

"Let's go sit down," Mason suggests right after the security guy lets me go.

His arm around my shoulders, he steers me toward a chair I didn't throw away. Sagging into the chair, my head in my hands, I fucking pray my failure didn't cost her her life.

# Chapter 7
## LAUREN

I've been going in and out of consciousness, all the while undergoing several tests. A mild concussion, a few bruises here and there, and a nasty cut on my right temple, which needed three stitches.

Apparently, I got lucky.

I wonder if it's a word I'll ever use again.

The party. The accident. I've relived every small detail too many times while falling in and out of sleep.

And, now that I finally have energy to get out of this place, Greg has decided to camp beside my bed.

If ten years of being around him wasn't enough for me to open up to him, then how does he expect me to let him back in after he tried to get rid of me this morning? Needless to say, he's wasting his time, sleeping in that uncomfortable chair.

"How long are you going to keep this up?" he asks as he opens his eyes.

I quickly twist my head and shut my eyes even though my pretend-to-sleep mode is useless now. He saw me staring. It doesn't change the fact that I have nothing to say. I'm stubborn. Sad enough, it's a trait we share.

I keep my eyes averted, biting my lip hard. As much as I don't want to acknowledge his presence, I need to find out where my sister is, and since I can't see my phone lying around, he's my best option.

"How is Kate?" I demand with a fierce look when I notice the dark bags under his eyes.

"Lauren," he whispers, his voice quavering as his hand reaches out to touch mine.

I pull it away before he has a chance to grab hold of it.

"Just tell me where she is," I utter. And, when he doesn't answer, I add, "You might as well leave if you can't even give me that."

"Stop pushing me away. I'm not—"

"Don't!" I lash out. I can't stand to hear one more word. "I heard you," I continue, my voice dangerously low.

"What?" His astonishment almost sounds sincere.

"I heard you," I repeat a little louder. "You want me gone."

He's about to deny it, I'm sure. But then he shakes his head. "You were listening." He pauses. "Is that why you ran away?"

"No," I bite back. "I don't need you." *Kate does.*

"Sending you away is for your own safety, Lauren."

I snort, my gaze flicking away from him while I'm breathing deeply. Not even this hospital gown will stop me from getting out of here if he keeps this up.

"There's this situation—"

"A situation?" I clip sarcastically as I snort. "Kate got shot, and someone ran me off the road. What the hell is going on?"

"I can't explain right now."

*So, he does know.*

"I just need you out of town. Stay with a friend of mine. It'll be temporary until everything's resolved," he stammers, as if every word is something he needs to think about.

He's talking in riddles, hiding things from me. And, even though I want to know badly, I refuse to beg. I'll figure it out myself.

So, I mutter, "Thank you, but no thanks."

"I'm not giving you a choice," he booms.

Although it really isn't our first argument, it's the first time I get goose bumps from the tone of his voice.

"Your safety isn't up for discussion," he vows, his eyes locked on mine.

"My safety is none of your concern," I snap.

He sighs deeply before he turns around, looking outside. "You can't leave this room."

My hands balling into fists, the inner child in me speaks up, "You can't stop me."

Turning around, he ignores my threat. "There's a guard outside your door," he calmly informs me.

Shifting my gaze to the door and then back on him, a loud, "What?" escapes my mouth. Cursing the fact that he's a cop, I shove the sheets out of the way. "You can't do this!"

And, when he remains unfazed, I manage to rip out my IV before he snatches my arms in a firm grip, shaking them.

"They ran you off the road, for Christ's sake."

My eyes bore into his. I already regret telling him that fact. It makes all of this much harder.

"For once, make the right decision," he growls, his fingers digging deeper into my skin.

As much as I pull my arms back, he doesn't let go, shattering the thought of him not being an abuser, reminding me of Jimmy—my mother's crazy ex-lover—who had his hands on me one too many times.

"Don't. Touch. Me."

A flicker of shock crosses his face before he lets go, and I scoot to the edge of the bed. My heart is hammering in my chest while an accelerating beeping sound resonates through the room. Every beep tears through my body, challenging my heart to go even faster, making me so agitated that I can't do anything but pull the clip off my finger.

"Lauren, I didn't mean to …" he says with so much pain in his voice, his hands reaching out again.

Not able to bear another touch, I jump out of bed, eyes on him as I retreat until my back is against the wall. My chest rising and falling heavily, I take another glimpse at the door. A way out. But, if what Greg said is true, someone else is waiting for me outside.

"Why are you doing this?" I fume, my eyes back on him.

He knows that I hate being cornered.

As he stays on his side of the bed, his hands clenched into fists, his eyes fill up with tears before he opens his mouth. "I can't lose you, too, Lauren."

His words sift through before I stammer, "Kate?"

As he shakes his head, his eyes full of unshed tears, it hits me. My legs giving out, I crash to the ground.

Shot down.

Not by a bullet, but the excruciating truth—the confirmation that my sister isn't somewhere in a hospital, fighting for her life.

Breathing.

# Chapter 8
## LIAM

I gaze at Lauren through the rearview mirror. She's in the middle seat, her head lolling to the side, as she's asleep.

Apart from her concussion and her stitched-up wound, which she got from hitting her head multiple times against the side of the car when it tumbled around, she's fine, living and breathing another day.

Five minutes.

That's how long I felt relieved when the doctors told me before it was replaced with bitterness and anger. I was seconds away from marching into her room and knocking some damn sense into her.

I would have.

But Mason physically stopped me, forced me to get in line. I wasn't the only one who wanted a word. Greg went in first, doing enough damage to cover all of us, and I never got my turn. I could only observe when I went in right after a nurse rushed into her room. Mason didn't even bother stopping me. He just followed me, halting right next to me to see Lauren slumped against the wall, eyes dull, completely broken because of something Greg had said. Or done.

I clutch the steering wheel harder, cursing Matthew and Mason for getting in between me and Greg. Because of them, I've got a vicious rage buried deep inside my chest. One I tend to keep there, so I can finish this job properly.

A job I would've quit if it wasn't for Matthew. He's the reason I'm sitting in this car, being the driver, instead of relaxing on a beach, taking my much-needed vacation.

*"I need you," Matthew insisted.*

*Gazing outside, I kept my eyes fixed on the trees in front of the hospital.*

*"They tried to kill her."*

*Turning around, I slammed my hand against the wall as I closed my eyes. "I don't need a fucking reminder."*

*"Apparently, you do."*

*"Kate's dead," I said in a gruff tone as I pushed off the wall, pointing a finger at myself. "On my watch."*

*"It wasn't your fault."*

*"Lauren slipped away, only to get driven off the road." I jabbed my index finger a little harder against my chest. "On my watch."*

*"Liam." His hand landed on my shoulder, and he squeezed hard. "It. Wasn't. Your. Fault." He emphasized every word. "If you really need a scapegoat, then blame me. I should have done it my way. But Vance didn't ask for private security; he wanted us to monitor them without them knowing. And, since he never received any real threats, I agreed."*

*Not my fault.*

*And yet, the only thing I could think about was that I. Had. Fucked. Up.*

*I shrugged off his arm and turned around.*

*"I need you, Liam."*

*"Your team can handle it."*

*"Colin and Dean"—two operatives of the SPISe Critical Response Unit—"are staying here to help with the investigation. I need you."*

*My gaze fixed on the ceiling, I cursed the fact that it was Matthew standing in front of me.*

*"Just help us get her to New York safely."*

*And, even though he was asking me something, he never posed a question. He already knew I would never be able to refuse.*

*"I have one condition," I agreed, facing him. "I'm driving."*

*Even though I knew Matthew hated being a passenger, he didn't hesitate to say, "Thank you."*

I bet he's regretting his decision right about now as he sits in the passenger seat, about to rip the ceiling handle off with the way he's pulling it down.

Ironic how we've all had to make our own sacrifices, including Mason, who got the job of handling Lauren, as he's sitting right next to her. Although he hasn't done much since she's been cooperating without any objection.

Not. One. Word.

And I can't fucking stand it.

# CHAPTER 9
## VANCE

*Ten Years Ago*

My head lying back, my feet propped up on the desk, I'm seriously considering sleeping right here, in my cramped desk chair, trying to forget this fucked up day, when the phone starts ringing.

It's past ten in the evening, and since it's not my cell phone, I can assume it's work-related, reason enough to just let it ring. Tomorrow is another day.

Yet someone's very persistent. And the plug is out of reach while the phone itself is at arm's length. Rolling my chair a little closer to the desk, I pick up and listen to whoever is calling. It can't get much worse than what I've been through.

"Mr. Newman?" a woman asks, uncertainty quavering in her voice.

Normally, I'm thrilled to have a woman calling me, but somehow, I get the feeling this isn't a booty call. "Yes?"

"I'm sorry to bother you so late this evening," she starts off.

If she expects me to reassure her that's not the case, then she's calling the wrong guy.

"I don't know how to do this—"

"Lady, I'm having a bad fucking day. Just say whatever you have to say, or we can end this call and both get along with our business."

She takes a deep breath before she continues, "Do you know a Summer Miller?"

I usually don't remember the names of the women I've been with. Yet her name hasn't left my mind.

"Summer Miller," she repeats. "She's from Wilmington."

A neighborhood I rarely visit. But I did make a house call a long time ago, ending up in a tavern afterward. That was where I found her, sitting at the bar, her long brown hair draped over her shoulder, her beautiful green eyes red and puffy, as she was sipping a white martini.

"Sir?" the woman on the other end chimes.

"Yes?"

"Do you know her, Mr. Newman?"

I deflect her question with a more prying one. "What does she want?"

"Well, I'm sorry to say this." She pauses briefly, sucking in a deep breath, before she adds, "But she passed away."

I take in her words while I remember how Summer slept in my arms that night, her lush brown hair smelling of roses, her gorgeous body against mine.

I've had my share of beauties, but she was different. And, even though she had a load of emotional baggage, I could see her potential, sense her fierceness. If I had been looking for a woman in my life, she would've been an excellent candidate. But, back then and even now, I can't get attached, not in my line of work. So, I treated her like every other woman in my life. I left and never returned. But, now, hearing that she's dead, it hits me in the chest.

"How?"

"She was in a car accident."

The image of someone slamming into her car starts playing out in my mind.

"Did someone hit her?" I bark. And, when she doesn't answer immediately, I shoot another question. "Did they find the bastard?"

"There was no one." She pauses. "She drove herself into a tree. She was drunk."

I don't know why I had to torture myself by asking. But, now, I have the confirmation that her issues got the best of her.

I could start playing the what-if game, but deep down, I know she would've never been safe with me.

Trying my best to shrug off the guilt, I lose my last chunk of patience, knowing there's nothing left for me to do. "Why are you calling?"

"Well, I know it's far-fetched and—"

"Tell me."

"We got an anonymous call from someone who claimed that you're the father of Summer's twins."

I've had a few calls like this, desperate women who wanted to have a second date, who wanted to draw me in by saying I'd impregnated them. I usually laugh my ass off, but again, in this case, it's different. I can only hold my breath as realization sets in.

We didn't use protection; she'd persuaded me to do it without a condom, assuring me that she was on birth control. And I'd believed her.

"I'm sorry I bothered you with this when I have no clue if that person was telling the truth. But she sounded so sure. And I know that, if there's no family, these two beautiful girls are destined for foster care, so I had to give this ... you ... a shot."

*Two girls.*

The lump in my throat grows to the size of a football.

"Sir?"

"I can't help you. Good luck in finding them a home." And, right after that, I end the call.

I couldn't even wait for her to say good-bye, afraid that, if the call lasted a second longer or she persisted more, I would've made another decision.

A dangerous one.

I can't.

Although I have to refrain from picking up the phone and calling back, I remind myself that I'm a private investigator. I get mixed up with vengeful people on a daily basis. My scarred chest and my broken hand are painful reminders.

I can't do this.

I have to let them go.

Yet, somehow, I'm afraid it'll be just like it was with their mom.

Impossible to forget.

# Chapter 10
## LAUREN



*Present*

I've taken my freedom for granted.

Now that it's been blown to pieces, I'm forced to rely on others to put it back together when, only a week ago, I would've fought tooth and nail to keep my independence.

But people change.

I've changed.

Drastically.

The people I've been avoiding for weeks—*him*, Mason, and Matthew, a tall, good-looking man who introduced himself as the brother of Mason—are friends with Greg, and they are hell-bent on helping him by taking me home with them.

I couldn't care less. Not even about the fact that I'm leaving behind my personal stuff, college, Amy.

It's all meaningless without *her*.

And then there's the funeral no one is talking about. I don't have the strength to ask, much less sit in a church with *her* in a box.

*I can't.*

Instead, I swallow down the pills they gave me, the ones that keep me from completely falling apart, another reason I'm absolutely compliant as they push me into a car and drive me to a private airstrip. Why I board their private jet and fly to New York. Why I follow them into an awaiting car after we landed.

All of it without any resistance while they all handle me as if I were made out of glass.

Except for *him*.

He's the only one who hasn't said a word, who's been driving, his shoulders rigid, his hands tightened around the wheel, eyes—visible at all times since he's not wearing his cap any longer—solely focused on the road ahead. Only a handful of glances my way, every single one filled with distaste, as if I were a contagious disease, one he's afraid of catching just by looking at me.

"We're almost home," Mason says, giving my thigh a gentle squeeze.

*Home.*

Staring out the dark tinted windows, the skyscrapers flashing by, I know this jungle of steel will never be my home.

Besides, I've never had one, and if I did, it's definitely gone now.


We drive into an underground garage of an all-glass skyscraper where only someone with a badge and a code can get in before we park right in front of the elevator.

"Why aren't we going up to her room?" Mason asks Matthew as we step into the elevator.

Matthew seems a bit older or more experienced, a leader with the way he's been telling everyone what to do since we left the hospital.

"I'll explain when we're in the conference room," he says, resolved, while he punches the button for the fortieth floor. Once there, Matthew flicks his hand. "Follow me."

We all pile out of the elevator and through a long hallway until we stop in front of two frosted glass doors with the letters *SPISe* cut out.

When Matthew swipes his card, the doors open, and I walk into a huge meeting room with a stunning city view, a giant oval glass table, and over thirty futuristic chairs that fill up the entire space in front of me.

Matthew motions for me to take a seat, and exhausted as I am, I plop down.

"What's going on?" Mason asks Matthew as he takes the chair on my right.

Walking a bit further away, he turns to us, his hands grabbing hold of the chair in front of him, his expression pained. "Vance wants to talk to her."

Mason opens his mouth when a hard voice on my left speaks up, "Hell. No." Even though *he* doesn't yell, he pronounces both words with absolute determination.

"Liam," Matthew says with a stern yet unsurprised voice, "I don't like it either, but I have no choice."

"You do have a choice. You tell him no," *he* says harder, slamming his hand on the table a few feet to my left, making me jump a little in my seat.

"He'll come and—"

"Let him. He won't get very far," he threatens.

The hair on the back of my neck springs to life.

*Is he defending me?*

"You know I can't stop him if he does. And, even if I could, there's still the fact that he'll draw unwanted attention our way."

"You think she's up for this?" Mason interrupts, his worried eyes shifting to me.

"No. But the decision isn't ours to make." Matthew rubs a hand over his face before his eyes zero in on me. "Lauren?"

I look up at him.

*What does he want me to say?*

I'm clueless.

"Do you think you can manage a quick phone call? There's someone who wants to talk to you."

"I thought I just heard you say that I have no choice." I point out the obvious.

"If someone has the right to say no, it's you," Matthew says before he suggests, "We'll postpone it."

*Postpone.*

I'll have to do it anyway, and I know that, once they give me a room and a bed, I won't have the strength to get back up.

"I'll do it. Ten minutes, tops. I'm tired," I demand, figuring Vance is just another cop who wants to know about my car accident. I've had to repeat my story only about a hundred times.

"All right, I'll check if he's available. I'll be right back."

Matthew walks past me when *he* seizes his right arm. Not a word is said as they face off, the whole room filling up with a dangerous tension so thick that it's almost hard to breathe.

Mason slowly rises from his chair, about to defuse the situation, when *he* releases Matthew's arm with a chuck before he turns around and stomps out of the room.

I really have no idea what his problem is. And, since there's enough drama in my life as it is, I focus on Matthew who reenters and sets up a conference call on a huge television screen hanging from the wall, facing the doors, on the other side of the table.

"We'll leave you alone to talk. If there's anything you need, just call," Matthew says, pointing to a phone attached to the wall a few feet to the right before he exits the room with Mason.

My eyes set on the television screen, I walk along the floor-to-ceiling-windows, taking a seat a bit closer to the screen, as a man with combed-back brown hair and a short, trimmed beard fills up the screen.

He intensely watches me, and I give him the same treatment.

"Hi, Lauren. I'm Vance Newman," he says while tapping his fingers on the desk in front of him. "Did you have a good flight?"

Digging my nails into the palm of my hand, I stare at him, dumbfounded.

"Are they treating you right?"

*I can't believe they interrogate people this way now.*

"Look, you wanted to talk. Get to the point."

*You've got only nine minutes left.*

"I see you've inherited my temper," he says, earning my undivided attention.

*What did he just say?*

And, while I'm busy discarding his implication, he confirms my worst nightmare.

"Lauren, I don't know how to say this, but"—he pauses—"I'm your father."

All my life, I've prepared myself for this sentence, this moment when someone steps up to me and says those words.

All my life, I've been practicing on how to respond.

That's why I say it without hesitation as I look him straight in the eye, "I have no father."

One sentence that carries years of pain from the hurt of being dumped by a parent, unwanted, as if having a twin were just something you could run from.

"Tests prove otherwise."

Not the answer I was expecting. And, while groveling would've been annoying, being cocky about it *really* isn't an option.

"What is it that you want from me? A kiss? A hug? You're not even brave enough to face me for real. Or would you rather I say that I've missed you and that I've been waiting my whole life for you, *Daddy*," I spit out before I take a deep breath. "I'm sorry to burst your bubble, but you're too late for your parental duties. You had your chance when we were born, and you left us. I'm a grown woman now, no thanks to you. I definitely don't need a father anymore," I finish without breaking eye contact.

I jump off my chair, my back to him, eyes set on the New York skyline.

He doesn't need to see my pain, nor the tears that threaten to spill as I think about the only person who would've wanted to meet him.

"I never meant to leave you."

Another direct hit, but I realize there's really nothing he could say that wouldn't make my blood boil. Only my sister's voice in my head keeps me from ending the call. I know she would've given him a chance regardless.

"I'm sorry," he says. "Now is probably not the time to get into that. And I *should've* done this in person. I would have, if the circumstances were different. I just wanted to see that you were okay," he says with so much guilt in his voice.

"Okay?" I shriek, turning around. "Yes, I'm perfectly fine. So lucky to be alive while …" I choke on my own sarcasm. I can't even say her name out loud. Tears roll down my cheeks when flashes of memories hit me like a freight train.

"I'm so sorry."

Another apology, his expression tormented.

"I knew I had a dangerous job, that I had to keep you away from me. I let Greg raise you, so you'd never be in danger. So you'd never get hurt. All of it, for nothing—"

"What?" I bristle, taking a step closer to the screen.

"I killed Enrico Powell. I had to. It was him or me. But his uncle, Frank Calvetti, he's …" He doesn't finish his sentence, searching for the right word. "He's a bad man; I knew that. So, I hired people to look out for you two, keep you safe. Frank couldn't have known that you two were mine. He shouldn't have known—"

He's babbling, forcing my mind to process all this information as his words slowly seep in. He's giving me an explanation for everything that has happened, offering me a person I can blame.

Because this man—this person who donated a part of his DNA, who never talked to us, never acknowledged our existence in any way—is responsible.

A series of shallow breaths leaves my mouth before I lose it completely.

Before a rage I've rarely felt takes over my whole body.

"This is your fault," I hiss as I walk up to the screen.

"Lauren—"

Even though I want him to hurt as much as I do, I can't stand to look at his face a second longer, so I end the call right before I slam my fist against the screen.

Yet it's not enough.

I have to get rid of it all.

I don't care about how the screen is attached to the wall, only that it has to come off. So, I grasp it above and below, and then I start pulling on the damn thing when I hear commotion in the room.

When I've managed to detach the screen from the wall, I turn around, screen in hand, and see Mason at the head of the table.

"Stop," he pleads, a frown across his forehead. And he's not the only one.

*He* comes in next, eyes blazing, his distress on full display, followed by Matthew, who wears a stern look.

And they're all facing *me*.

What a sight I must be, a giant screen in my hands, tears coursing down my cheeks, yet I couldn't care less.

My head held high, I stare at their frozen bodies when I start to realize. "You knew!"

"Gorgeous," Mason pleads.

No denial.

"You all knew, and you didn't tell me!"

Nobody says a word. Not one.

"Fuck. You. All!" I scream right before I smash the TV on the floor.

Looking back up, I see how they're moving in on me. Mason comes straight for me while *he* takes the right side along the table.

"Gorgeous, stop. You're going to hurt yourself," Mason pleads.

"Matthew!" *he* roars a hidden message before Matthew leaves the room.

"I don't care," I chant over and over, not bothered that I'm acting like a crazy woman.

*Why would I?*

They took away my freedom while they kept the truth hidden. And, now, I'm left to deal with this unbearable fact, this undeniable need to destroy, while I'm stuck in a room with almost nothing to throw or trash.

Just one giant table.

One huge plate of glass.

Too smooth.

Too perfect.

I have to shatter it, break it into a million pieces.

I eye the chair at the head of the table before I stare back at Mason and *him*. Although they're both getting closer, they won't be able to stop me in time, considering the size of the table.

"Lauren," Mason begs, his hands up in the air, taking slow steps my way.

Disregarding his plea, I do the only thing that'll help with the searing pain inside of me. I grab the white leather chair in front of me—its metal legs the perfect weapon for what I'm about to do—before I lift it as high as I possibly can.

"Don't do it," *he* hisses, gracing me with his first three words.

Another useless attempt to stop me from doing this, from using my whole body weight to smash the chair into the table.

The inevitable happens.

The plate shatters on impact, but by giving it my all, I lose my balance, too.

Normal people would brace themselves, would scream, but I'm not normal anymore. I just let myself fall, yearning to feel anything apart from the agonizing pain that fills me inside out.

And I do as I bump my head against something solid before I smack onto the floor that is covered with thousands of tiny glass fragments.

Lying among the debris, I am exactly like the table—crumbled into a million pieces. I'll never fit together again.

Completely useless.

And, even though my body gives me all kinds of distress signals, I just lie here, utterly motionless but fully conscious to hear everything happening around me.

"Are you okay?" Mason asks, kneeling beside me.

Hands touch my body, and my vision shifts from the window to the ceiling, my body rolling on its back.

"Call an ambulance!" *he* yells to someone else entering the room before I notice him on my other side, his eyes zeroing in on something above my head. "Does your head hurt?"

Even though I try to focus on anything but *him*, I can't help but notice that, for the first time, his eyes display something else, and his touch is soft and caring.

"Gorgeous, where does it hurt?" Mason asks, brushing a strand of hair out of my face.

Although I hear every question, feel every touch, I'm completely lost in time and space.

"Where is that fucking ambulance?" *he* roars, his eyes skimming over my body once more, before he makes a decision. "I'm getting you out of here."

*What? No!*

I want to stay right here. I'm afraid that, when they start to move me, I'll lose this numbness. "Leave me be," I whisper as I push a hand to his chest.

"You're lying on pieces of glass," *he* snaps, ignoring my wish as he tries to slide his arms beneath my body.

"I don't care," I rip out.

I try to get away from *him*, but Mason's on the other side.

"Gorgeous, let us take care of you."

"No." I shake my head as more tears make their way down my cheeks. "Leave me alone," I plead before I make another attempt to scramble away while flailing my arms to prevent them from getting ahold of me.

But I'm outnumbered.

I'm too weak to stop *him* from changing positions as he snakes his arms around my upper body before pinning down my arms while he pulls me against his chest.

So fixed on fighting back, I only notice at the very last moment that Matthew's back, and he's close, holding something in his hand. My shirt and sweater are pulled out of the way, and I feel a sting along my upper arm, followed by a warm sensation slowly spreading throughout my whole body.

*Matthew.*

He gave me a shot of something.

I gaze at him when I notice a syringe in his hand.

"Everything's going to be fine," Mason assures me.

*He* shifts his hold—one arm beneath my knees, the other around my back—lifting me off the ground.

"Why couldn't you just leave me alone?" I slur as I stare into *his* eyes.

I'd rather scream it to him, fight his hold, but instead, numbness overpowers every cell of my body while my question remains unanswered. A look of guilt is plastered all over his face.

*They gave me a freaking sedative.*

As if lying wasn't bad enough, they now want to control my every move.

Literally stung by their betrayal, I close my eyes as I know more than ever that I'm truly on my own.

# Chapter 11
## VANCE

*Three Days Ago*

"Get me a secure line and call Matthew," I order once my crew and I have entered the offices. "Now."

I refuse to accept that I've made the wrong decision about the only choice in my life that was almost impossible to make.

It took me weeks before I decided to refuse fatherhood, to let them go. Before I found them Greg—an LAPD detective who'd already raised his son into a decent young man when his wife died—who was capable of giving them a safe and warm home while I stayed out of their lives, which was much harder than I ever could've expected.

Yet I hid in the shadows, for them, for their safety.

A complete stranger.

Who didn't have the right to tuck them into bed at night.

Who wasn't there to celebrate their birthdays.

Who didn't get to teach them how to drive a car.

Who couldn't take them to a shooting range and teach them how to defend themselves.

"Vance, are you there?"

Taking another deep breath, I grab hold of the phone Brad is holding out to me. "Where are they, Matthew?"

*Please tell me they're at home, in bed, on this Saturday night.*

"I got a distress call from Mason. Something's happened."

It's my worst nightmare, the one I wanted to avoid, and now, I have to suffer through it all while I'm miles away.

Unable to protect my own family.

My daughters.

# Chapter 12
## LIAM

*Present*

I could have walked away, turned my back, and left Lauren Miller in the hands of the Scott brothers. After all, I'd completed Matthew's favor.

Yet here I am, right in the middle of this mess, wanting to blame Matthew when I should really blame myself.

Nobody insisted that I stick around while she called her father.

No one forced me to be in that conference room when she was in full destruction mode.

Or asked me to carry her out when she lost it.

Yet that's exactly what I did.

Me and this irresistible urge to save her, and I'm losing my goddamn mind over her actions.

"She's going to be all right," Mason assures me.

The elevator doors reveal his apartment, and I carry her in.

*How many times will he have to reassure me of that when I have her lifeless body in my arms while I fret over her sanity?*

I had one condition to get her here. I'd be the driver.

But then I barged into the conference room, and when I saw Lauren standing there—screen in hand, eyes bright red, tears rolling down her cheeks—I saw it for the first time.

Her vulnerability.

Even though I had been there when Lauren found Kate bleeding out on the floor, I had been so busy trying to save

Kate that I couldn't focus on Lauren's pain or see how she was falling apart.

But, today, I stood face-to-face with a Lauren who wasn't hiding her sadness or her pain.

Every emotion was on full display.

How I wanted her to run to me.

I would've caught her.

But, even if I were her last resort, she would never.

I've seen enough of her over the past few months to know she needs her space, craves independency. That's why I stayed back, forced to witness how she hurt herself. I really should've denied her self-reliant tendencies, ignored her need for distance. I could've stopped her from smashing that table and getting herself hurt.

Placing her onto the bed, I run a hand through her hair, finding the bump on the back of her head from hitting one of the metal table bars. "She hit her head pretty bad."

"She's going to be fine," Mason says, sitting on her other side.

I don't know if it's me or himself that he's trying to convince. But it's clear that he cares. A lot. He's gotten attached to her in a way I'm still trying to figure out. I shouldn't feel threatened by my best friend when I have no claim on her whatsoever, but I can't help it. I can't control myself around her.

"The paramedics are here," Matthew states, entering the room after a brief knock.

"Send them in."

*I want to hear them say the words Mason's been saying over and over.*

"She's got a good pupil reflex, and her vitals are good," the paramedic confirms once he's done examining Lauren.

"What about her head?"

"It's hard to diagnose when she's unconscious. But the fact that she didn't lose consciousness or throw up right after her fall is a good sign. Just keep her monitored throughout the night. I would wake her up every two hours once the sedation has worn off. And, if she feels nauseous or dizzy or if she has a serious headache, I would recommend another scan. Otherwise, a checkup from a doctor in the morning will suffice."

It's not at all what I wanted to hear, and my mind is still freaking out when the paramedic and Matthew leave Mason and me alone in her room.

"I'll sleep in here tonight," I say, resolved, as I can't keep my eyes off her unmoving body.

"We'll set up another bed," Mason proposes, rising from the bed.

"And we need to remove as much as possible." I motion to the paintings and the other clutter in the room. "I don't trust her with all this shit around."

*Fuck.*

I don't even trust her to be by herself with absolutely nothing in her room.

I don't know what she's capable of or how she'll deal with her sister's death.

But I know one thing.

She won't hurt herself again.

Not when I'm around.

# CHAPTER 13
## LAUREN

*Five Weeks Later*

The December rain pours furiously against my window, making me wonder if it's as cold as it looks from the inside out.

Yet I wouldn't know since I haven't been outside these past few weeks. Too busy sleeping, eating, and showering.

If it were up to me, it would be even more simplistic, but according to certain people, my opinion is irrelevant.

Of all the friends Greg could've asked for me to go to, it had to be Matthew Scott, son of Elliot Scott, who is the owner of Scotts' Private Investigation and Security, a privately owned security company with offices across the world. That's how I ended up here, at the company's head office—or well, an apartment above the company—in downtown New York.

No room for negotiation.

No room to hide.

Mason and *he* have arranged everything, setting me up in this enormous bedroom with a television and one extra bed next to mine—because they've also decided I can't sleep by myself. Normally, *he* keeps me company at night. But, this past week, Mason has had babysitting duty.

Basically, I have zero privacy. And, once again, I'm reminded of that when *he* barges in while I'm lying in bed, my shirt and pajama shorts still on even though it's almost noon.

Without glancing my way, he walks straight past my bed to the built-in closet on the opposite side of the room. Pulling out my duffel bag, he starts dragging my clothes—which someone delivered shortly after I arrived here—off their hangers and throws them on top of the bag.

Needless to say, he's got serious issues.

"Liam!" Mason yells right before he enters the room, slightly out of breath, his gaze darting from me to *him.* His shoulders sag a little in relief. "What are you doing?"

*What is he doing? But, if it involves me leaving this place, I'm all in.*

"Liam," he stresses again, taking a step closer while *he* continues his onslaught.

"She needs to go."

For once, I totally agree. Mason, not that much.

"What?"

"I refuse to wait until she's no more than a skeleton. She needs help."

*I might have lost a few pounds, but it's not that bad.*

"She sees a therapist every week," Mason reminds *him.*

*Sadly.*

*He* halts, turns around, and gives Mason this incomprehensible look.

"Dr. Jemerson? What has he done these past few weeks? Nothing's changed. Does he even look at her while he's talking?" he yells, pointing a finger at me. "A vegetable is more alive than she is!"

*A vegetable? Really?*

Still, Mason shifts his eyes to me while *he* doesn't wait for an answer. Instead, he shoves the pile of clothes into the bag.

"I'm taking her to the hospital. At least there, I know her body will get what it needs."

I've been an excellent observer. Until now.

"No way," I shriek. I'm not going back to the hospital, anywhere but *that* place. Stomping the sheets out of the way, I shift my butt to the side of the bed, my gaze fixed on Mason, pleading for him to stop this insanity.

"We'll arrange another checkup with her doctor," Mason suggests.

*Another checkup.*

It's been a while since I had one. I've been quite good at hiding my lack of appetite, and I've been wearing a lot of baggy clothes. I'm not fooling anyone, especially *him.* And, even though this room is far from ideal, a hospital bed would suffocate me more.

"I'll try harder," I murmur when I look Mason in the eye.

The only reasonable person in the room.

He gives me a long stare before he sets his eyes on *him.* "Give her until Monday."

Five days to boot my life back into something normal is impossible.

Five days to get them to believe I'm getting better is worth a shot.

# Chapter 14
## LAUREN

Day four, and I'm trying. I really am.

I've been eating more. I've even joined them at the table for almost every single meal.

But the thing about pretending is that I need a way to cope, a way to hide the darkness threatening to cripple me into a shadow of myself. Simply existing inside this building isn't the way. I need to get out, breathe in oxygen I don't just exhale. If only they shared my opinion.

I'm sprawled across the long couch. The floor-to-ceiling windows display a starless night sky above the city skyline. The darkness of the outside lurks with only a plate of glass separating me from the outside world.

Looking around the spacious living and kitchen area, I don't see anyone even though I just had dinner with Mason and Sarah, Matthew's girlfriend.

I'm all alone.

A rarity, and it urges me even more to find a way out.

Walking up to the elevator, I inspect the keypad. It's more complex than the regular ones. Yet I wouldn't expect any less from a privately owned security company. This skyscraper is the modern version of a fortress. Still, it doesn't stop me as my finger is about an inch away from a button when I hear someone behind me.

"Lauren," a female voice speaks up.

Turning around, I look at Sarah, who's still wearing her dress suit—as Matthew's PA, she's probably obliged to wear something so formal—although her long blonde hair is no longer up in a tight bun but hanging loosely around her shoulders.

"I thought you'd left," I say out loud.

"I went to the restroom," she explains with guilt in her voice, as if going to the toilet is a crime.

I've seen her a few times since I arrived here. But these past few days, she came over to eat lunch and dinner with me, Mason, and *him*.

By now, I've come to learn that she's a gentle soul, worried about everything and everyone. Her feeling guilty about her visit to the restroom is yet another confirmation that she's too kind, too much like the only person I'm afraid to think about.

Turning my back to her, I press the red button that'll hopefully get me into the elevator.

"Lauren, don't do it. It's going to set off an alarm," she says, her voice full of distress.

Her warning doesn't stop me from jabbing a few more buttons before an alarm goes off, blaring through the living area.

"I'll call Matthew. I'll tell him I pushed the wrong button. Don't worry about it," she babbles. She comes up to stand next to me, reaching out for the phone hanging from the wall on the right side of the elevator.

Grabbing ahold of her outstretched arm, I tell her, "No." I refuse to involve her in my mess. "It's okay. You don't need to do anything."

"What's going on?" Mason demands, walking into the living room. "Sarah?" he questions her while he focuses on my hand, which is still holding on to her arm.

Mason, as overprotective as ever.

Even though I respect him for it, it pains me to see the doubt in his eyes. I would never hurt her, let alone for my own benefit.

"Everything's fine." She shrugs, her voice nullifying her message.

"I want to go out." I turn back to the elevator, ready to break open these damn metal doors if necessary.

As if the elevator received my telepathic threat, the doors open, revealing *him*. Tension is written all over his face, anger defining every muscle in his exposed forearms, as his eyes zone in on me.

Although we've been around each other on a daily basis, him sleeping in a bed three feet away from mine, we've always kept a certain distance.

Until now.

Every step he takes forward is a step back for me. Completely unfair if you consider the fact that he's at least six inches taller than me. It's absolutely unbearable to have his body halting only a foot away. A clear attempt of intimidation, one I can't submit to.

Slightly shaking my head, I focus on Sarah's face and then Mason's, confirming I have everyone's attention.

It's the perfect opportunity to make my demand, and I carefully choose to say the words, "I need to go out." I don't want to give them the illusion that they've got a choice.

And yet, a simple, "No," escapes *his* mouth.

I look back at him, seeing his eyes are dead set on me, and my defying no gets stuck in my throat.

"Gorgeous, I don't think you're ready—"

Shifting my gaze toward Mason, who's further away from me, I'm able to tell him, "I. Am."

"You've been living in your bed for weeks. You're not going out," *he* states, as if he has the right or the power to ground me.

I glare back at him, disregarding his words, trying to be unimpressed by his body in front of me. But it doesn't change the fact that it's blocking my only way out.

"You've got no authority over me. I'm an adult. You—" I start to say with a raised voice, pointing a finger that is merely an inch away from stabbing his chest.

"I want a word with her," he huffs, cutting me off, his eyes gliding to Mason, ignoring me altogether.

"Liam," Mason objects.

"Alone," *he* barks back.

The word *danger* is flashing vividly in my mind, urging me to use their disagreement to step around *him*, but he grabs on to my arm.

Considering we haven't been this close and haven't touched at all since my breakdown in the conference room, his grip is firm.

"Out!" he snaps, still glaring at Mason.

A word I wish were directed at me.

I wouldn't hesitate like Mason does before he guides a worried Sarah into the elevator.

The minute we're alone, the second the doors slam shut, I try to take a step back, only to be pulled back on the spot.

"Let me go," I command, every word said with sheer determination.

"You want to go out, Lauren? You want to run away from this? From us? Get yourself killed?" he hisses.

His words hit my most vulnerable spot while my own words get stuck.

Actions take over, my free arm flying upward, my hand aching to smack his cheek.

It doesn't happen.

My hand halts midair, my wrist in his hand, as he continues his verbal onslaught.

"An adult?" he prods. "Well then, fucking act like one instead of acting like a goddamn child—running away from your problems, refusing help from others, denying what's right in front of you!"

Having ahold on both of my arms, he inches closer while I keep on shuffling backward.

"For the first time in months, you finally feel something, and what is the first thing you do? You run. Again!" he yells, emphasizing his last word.

By now, we've ended our little dance, as my back is against the wall, the space between our bodies almost nonexistent while my vision blurs into a red haze.

"What are you going to do, Lauren? You can't run. You can't hide. You can't be fucking numb and lifeless. What the hell are you going to do?" he bellows, releasing my arms and plastering both hands on either side of my head.

My emotions are running so high; I'm sure they're going to rip me apart when he presses his body up against mine.

While he's looking down on me, I feel his hot breath on my skin, his mouth dangerously close. I only need to push up to my toes to—

"What the hell?"

My heels touch the ground before I look at Mason, who's standing in the elevator, his wary eyes zeroing in on the both of us, and I realize I've got my hands on *his* hips.

As fast as lightning, I retract them, my eyes fixed on *his* shirt, my heart thumping a hard beat in my chest.

*What just happened?*

*He* slowly pushes himself off the wall, all the while retaining eye contact with Mason. It's the ideal moment for me to get away, and I scurry toward the elevator, joining Mason.

"Can you take me to Sarah?"

The perfect escape.

Even though I've been deflecting her good intentions, opening up to her seems to be a better option than staying behind with *him.*

With a worried glaze in his eyes, he nods, placing an arm around my shoulders, hugging me close to his body while the doors start to close again.

As if I haven't tortured myself enough, I look up to see *him.*

He's still frozen on the very same spot.

His hands curled into tight fists.

His mouth drawn into a thin line.

I can tell that he's hanging on by a nearly ripped thread.

# Chapter 15

## LAUREN

*Seven Months Ago*

"Who do we have here?" a male voice chimes behind me. An arm curls around my neck as he leans further down before he continues saying close to my ear, "Lauren and Kate Miller."

No need to turn around to confirm Paul the douche is back.

My sister, who's sitting next to me in the campus cafeteria, grabs ahold of my hand, signaling for me to stay put. She prefers to ignore rather than engage.

"What place should we go to on our first date?" he whispers in my direction, his bad breath hitting my nose.

Biting my tongue while tapping my fingers on the table, I remain unfazed. It's not the first time a guy has wanted to change my no-dating status. And it's definitely not the first time he's proposed.

"Or shall I go out with your beautiful sister?" Posing his question in Kate's direction, he removes his arm from around my neck, so he can switch all his attention to her.

*Thus far ignoring him.*

Scraping my chair along the cafeteria floor, I force him to step back as I rise to my full height—a whopping five feet five inches—but the package inside is what he should be afraid of.

Still, I'm willing to use words one more time, for Kate, before I consider actions. "Paul, I get that it's hard for you to get rejected by a girl who uses her mouth to talk. I understand. That's why I'll say it *one* more time." Raising one finger in the air, I indicate both me and my sister. "We can barely stand to share our personal space with you." I sigh, the reminder of his smelly breath still on my mind. "A date with Kate or me will *never* happen."

"Come on, Lauren. We could be so good together," he says overconfidently, winking at his friends across the cafeteria.

By now, Kate is standing beside me.

"But we all know, you and I," he starts to say with his eyes on Kate, "would be perfect."

Switching my position so that Kate is behind my back, I take the bait, enjoying the fact that he picked an overly crowded cafeteria to get his ass kicked by a girl. And, although I'd rather believe my body is imposing, it's really not when I'm in front of a tall frat boy. Then again, height isn't what makes you powerful; it's what you know and how you put it to use.

Greg forced Kate and me to take self-defense lessons even though I had taken one before that. A rather brutal lesson given by Jimmy—who had more interest in Kate and me than my mother—taught me all about standing up for myself.

Placing my hands on Paul's arms should be a first warning to him, one he misunderstands, according to the glee in his eyes.

*I'll make it crystal clear.*

Smiling back at him, I whip one of my legs out and kick him in his most vulnerable spot. A strange choking sound slips from his mouth as he stumbles back a little. His hands between his legs, he breathes heavily before he looks up and starts grinning at me.

A sly freaking grin.

I've got an arsenal of moves that I want to put into practice. But, all of a sudden, a male someone, baseball cap on backward, fills up my entire vision.

With a hand indicating for me to stay back, a voice grounds out, "Back off, Paul."

Mason Scott, the guy with an impeccable built-in douche radar, has come to the rescue. It isn't the first time he has interfered, and although I appreciate him looking out for my sister, I can handle myself just fine. So, I disregard Mason's hand motion while I step to his side.

"Mason? Dude, chill out! I'm giving these girls the opportunity of a lifetime," says Paul, the man who has drowned every brain cell with alcohol.

"Leave," Mason snarls.

Even though Mason is normally a lot like my sister when it comes to resolving issues, he's got his hand on Paul's chest, anger flaring across his face.

"What is it, Mason? Are you calling dibs?" Paul drawls. "Which one do you want? Kate's sweet. But Lauren, well, she's a feisty—"

An unfinished sentence.

First, Paul is in front of Mason.

One blink of an eye later, Paul's back is against the nearest concrete column, and he's being held in place by a tall, athletic guy with a burgundy baseball cap on his head. He's clutching the collar of Paul's sweater so hard; his knuckles turn white.

"Liam," Mason warns.

A warning the guy named Liam chooses to ignore.

"If I see you near them one more time, I swear, you won't be able to bother any girl. Ever. Again," he threatens.

Only when Paul manages to give a small nod does Liam release him with a chuck, shoving him toward the exit of the cafeteria.

Shuffling the first few steps, he walks off with two of his friends in tow while I shift my eyes to Liam, who just whipped that sleazy grin off of Paul's face.

He fixes his menacing, dark eyes on me, and shivers zip along my skin, urging me to take an involuntary step toward him.

*Who are you?*

Expecting something, really anything, I'm stunned to notice how he diverts his eyes, turns around, and walks off.

As I stare at his retreating back, I realize I've never been *this* intrigued by a guy.

One who dares me to get rid of my most sacred value.

Because the fact is, when it comes to guys, I never chase.

I run.

As fast as I can.

In the opposite direction.

# Chapter 16
## LAUREN



"What happened?" Mason prods the moment the elevator doors shut.

He's asking me something I can barely grasp.

"Lauren"—he takes hold of my chin, tilting my head up—"did Liam hurt you?"

"What?" I shake my head, realizing what he's asking. "No, he didn't," I say defensively, looking Mason in the eye.

With his hand on my skin and my cheeks still burning, I step away from his touch, retreating.

Mason takes one more look at me before he reaches out for the elevator phone. "Sarah, Lauren's with me. She wants to come up. Is that okay with you?"

I don't hear her response, but a minute later, we're entering another apartment, similar to Mason's. Except for the furniture, which is all wood-based.

"She was just about to take a shower. She won't be long," Mason informs me as I hurry out of the elevator, happy to be anywhere if it's away from *him.*

Only five minutes after I've taken a seat in their bow-shaped cream leather couch, I see Matthew walking into the apartment, looking rather unhappy with the way he strides toward the kitchen where Mason is rummaging through the cupboards.

I can't overhear what they're whisper-hissing, but I don't have to be a genius to know it's about me.

"Lauren, I'm going to be straight with you," Matthew says as he approaches me, still sitting on the couch. "I love Sarah, and I would do anything to keep her from getting hurt. That's why my conscience is pressuring me to say this to you." He pauses a few feet away from me. "It's absolutely not an option for her to get dragged into any situation where she'll get physically or emotionally hurt," he states, a clear threat hidden behind his words.

I get what he's saying. I might not care about myself, but I have no intention of dragging Sarah into my mess, especially now.

"You've got my word." I can't say much more, but somehow, that one sentence is enough.

Since Matthew has always been distant around me, I stand up from the couch before I continue, "I have an even better proposition. Just give me a way out of this." I gesture toward my surroundings. "And I'll be out of Sarah's life. You won't have to worry anymore," I vow as I realize it's the perfect solution for everyone.

Well, maybe not *everyone*.

My eyes shift to Mason in the kitchen as his protruding eyes tell otherwise.

Apparently, Matthew knows his brother through and through. Without so much as a look in Mason's direction, Matthew knows he has to temper his brother, and he does so with a small hand gesture, demonstrating once more how he's used to getting everyone under his control and that he's definitely earned his position as the head of the Critical Response Department.

"Lauren, I haven't had the time to get to know you. But my brother and Liam, who I consider a brother, have. They care about you."

I have to swallow that one down.

"Maybe I wasn't totally clear just now, but every family member is of high importance to me, and if they care about someone, they automatically matter to me, too." He lowers his hand as he steps closer, our bodies only two feet apart, as if he's making sure his words hit home. "If you so much as take a step out of this building, if that's even possible, I'll find you and bring you back. You leaving will never be the solution to any of your problems."

Message received.

If only I could digest it, embrace this family who has opened up their home for me. Yet I do what I do best. I deny it. All of it. I can't get attached to people who'll be out of my life once this threat has been resolved.

"Speaking of family, I know you're having a hard time. But Greg really would like to talk to you, if only by phone."

Shaking my head, I focus on the modern painting behind him as I try to ignore the countless frustrations that get triggered by the sound of his name.

He sent me here.

He wanted me gone.

He got his wish.

"I can't." It's the only response I can give Matthew. It's the only answer I've given my therapist about a hundred times.

"Let me know when you can." He nods.

"But I would like to call Amy." I haven't heard from her since that night. "Or maybe she can come over?"

"It isn't safe to reach out to her. Not for you. Or for Amy," he explains. "I'm sorry, Lauren." His eyes darken with sympathy. "Now, I have to get back to work," he says to Mason before he exits the apartment with his brother in tow.


"Hi, Lauren," Sarah greets as she walks into the living room, her blonde hair still wet. "Is everything all right?" she asks before she plops down next to my outstretched body.

"I'm fine, just a little tired."

A sympathetic smile crosses her face, proof that I'm hiding my true feelings pretty badly.

I need something to loosen me up, and Sarah's next question is the perfect solution to my problem.

"You want something to drink?"

Without hesitation, I speak up, "Alcohol." God, I sound like an addict, yet I don't care enough to change my mind. "Something with alcohol in it."

She rises slowly, shuffling on her feet before she speaks her mind, "I don't think it's smart to get drunk right now."

She's right.

"I guess one drink won't hurt." She turns around, going to a glass cabinet. "Maybe you should come and have a look. I don't drink much."

I smirk before I join her. Standing in front of Matthew's liquor cabinet filled with expensive bottles, I grab the first vodka bottle I see before I follow Sarah into the kitchen where she grabs two glasses and sets them on the counter. I pour myself a glass, and Sarah holds out hers.

"Are you sure?"

"Just a taste," she says.

That's all the encouragement I need to give her a quarter of the amount I took.

"Maybe you should add a little juice; it'll be tastier," I propose.

"That's okay. It won't be that bad," she says, raising her glass.

We clink our glasses before I gulp down a good amount while Sarah starts sipping from hers. Her crinkling nose and squinting eyes speak for themselves.

"A little fruit juice it is."


An hour and a half later, I truly regret my fruit-juice suggestion. She's been downing her vodka cocktail like it's lemonade, becoming this happy drunk who's too curious for her own good.

"So, Lauren, are you in love with Liam?" she asks bluntly.

Alcohol spurts out of my mouth.

"Or are you falling for Mason's charms?"

Still coughing up my drink, I manage to vigorously shake my head as I slam a hand on my chest. "Why the hell would you think I was involved with any of them?" I shriek when I finally swallow the liquor in my mouth.

Sober Sarah would've backed down, but I have the grace to meet drunken Sarah, who's quite relentless.

"Come on, Lauren. Who is it? They both insisted on letting you stay here, and since you're not family, there's only one possibility left." She shrugs, taking another sip from her glass.

And it'll be her last.

"I need another drink," I say more to myself as I confiscate the bottle.

"So, you don't want either of them?" She keeps pushing.

I take a big swig. "I don't want a guy in my life. Ever," I stress, hoping she'll back off now.

"Really?" She gasps. "How can you be happy without?"

*Nope, she absolutely doesn't get it.*

I fill my glass back up while she motions for me to fill hers, which I don't, for obvious reasons. The main one being Matthew, who'll kill me when he discovers she's drunk because of me.

"I mean, I wouldn't want to miss Matthew's—"

"Sarah!" I yell as I lift my hand. "I don't need to know. Really!"

"Love, Lauren. I was going to say love," she jokes.

I can't help but smile, if only a little.

"So, you don't want a boyfriend?"

I shake my head as I take another gulp.

*What can I say? It's a touchy subject.*

"Don't you believe in love?"

I sigh. "There's no such thing. Not for me."

"Why?"

She's lucky I'm drunk. The alcohol is doing a great job in making me softer.

"My mother. She wanted love, searched for it her entire life, and the only thing she found was misery and pain. I don't want to end up like her."

"Did she give up, too?"

It's a bad question, but she doesn't know that.

"She's dead. Got drunk and decided it was okay to drive. She crashed her car into a tree," I tell her frankly.

She stares at me, speechless for the first time, tears gathering at the corners of her eyes.

"I'm so sorry, Lauren."

*Sorry.*

The inevitable word everyone says. When the only person who needs to say it is no longer here.

"Don't be," I assure her, a bitter taste in my mouth while a familiar rage presses down on my chest. An everlasting feeling.

I've never cried over the death of my mother. But my sister, wearing her heart on her sleeve, was inconsolable for weeks. And, now, they're both gone, leaving me here to fend for myself. If it wasn't for the alcohol, I would be freaking out. Instead, I drink from the bottle while an awkward silence spreads throughout the room.

Sarah leaves the couch and stumbles away. Then, five seconds later, a pop song fills the living room.

"Music makes me happy," she explains as she dances to the rhythm of the song while she makes her way back to me.

So, we do have something in common. I must admit, I wouldn't have thought she was the dancing type of girl.

"I only do this at home," she slurs, as if reading my thoughts.

"Why?" I ask, still sitting on the couch, bottle in hand.

"I can't dance in public. People would laugh their asses off if they saw me dancing like this!" she yells a little too loud.

I bet they would crack a smile but not because she's ridiculous. No. Everyone would look at her with a genuine smile on their face as they got to see a glimpse of her happiness, her innocence, while being jealous of this rarity in our current society. I know I am. I love to dance, but it's more of a way to get out my frustrations.

"Come on, Lauren, dance with me!" she urges, crawling onto the wooden coffee table.

I don't feel much like dancing, but refusing her would be like ignoring a puppy in distress. So, I join her as I keep the bottle in hand, and I pray the wooden table is solid enough to support the both of us. Remarkably, Sarah isn't worried at all.

We're both a little lost in the moment, and that's how we fail to notice the growing audience.

Only when Sarah stops her swirly moves before jumping off the table do I turn my buzzed head to see her running into Matthew's arms. Then, my eyes focus on the person next to him, the one who still has a stony glare carved into *his* dark eyes.

I swear, he's got a sixth sense for the worst timing ever when I'm involved.

Matthew lifts Sarah off the ground and cradles her in his arms before she lets him carry her out of the living room.

*If he thinks he can do the same to me, he can think again.*

I get off the table and let myself fall onto the couch. Now more than ever, I have the need to consume more alcohol. But the bottle never reaches my lips. One second, it was in my hand, and a second later, it's gone.

"You've had enough," *he* barks as he inspects the bottle and the amount I haven't downed.

Since there's not much left, I leave him this small victory. I grab the remote next to me and turn on the TV as I hear him pouring the liquor into the sink.

While he's wandering around in the kitchen, I drift off, not caring how or when I'm going to end up in my bed.

But I know it's very likely that he'll make sure I do.

# Chapter 17
## LAUREN

My throat feels sore, and my head is drumming to a beat that is no longer there.

The aftermath of alcohol.

I'm forced to pay the price for those few moments when I didn't feel suffocated by the awful memories.

But my body's condition isn't what is bothering me most; it's the fact that I'm still in Matthew and Sarah's apartment, on their couch, exactly where I fell asleep.

Still dark outside, I have no clue what time it is when I drag myself up and away from their lounge, my body mocking me with every step while my stubbornness pushes me in the direction of the elevator.

"Screw this." I feel lucky right now, my finger going to the keypad to push in the first combination that comes to mind.

*Incorrect.*

"I wouldn't do that if I were you," Matthew threatens.

I push in another code.

At my second attempt, he asks, "How old are you again?"

I don't know how people mistake stubbornness or independency for childish behavior. Or is it because I'm a woman that I have to automatically listen to every man in my life say what I can and cannot do?

"Old enough to make my own decisions," I declare as a second *Incorrect* flashes across the screen.

"Age isn't something that makes you able to handle everything that comes your way. Sometimes, you have to rely on others."

*Says the man who clearly hasn't been dumped by anyone.*

Still, I must admire Matthew's persistence, his professionalism.

*He* would've been riled up already.

"I've done fine on my own," I spit out.

A truth I've always believed in, but now, it just burns a hole into my soul, the smoke filling my lungs with every breath I take as my vision starts to breed black spots.

"Let me get you back to the apartment," Matthew states as he comes to stand in front of me, pushing in the code while blocking the screen with his body.

And, since I'm too busy keeping myself in an upright position, I can only follow him back to the apartment.

Digesting his words in a way I know best.

Deny. Deny. Deny.

# Chapter 18
## LIAM

*What the hell am I still doing here?*

I've been asking myself that very same question for too long.

The plan was to help transfer her safely here and leave right after.

But I've stayed. Convinced she would get through this and come out differently. Smarter. More careful.

Wishful thinking—or rather, irrational thinking.

Today's actions have confirmed the contrary. She's back to her old habits. Trying to run off, only four days after she got out of her bed. Flirting her way out when I cornered her, so she could run off with Mason.

And, of course, her being Lauren Miller, she couldn't stop there; she had to finish this whole fucking mess with getting Sarah and herself drunk.

How I wanted to swing her over my shoulder and get her back to her room to shake some sense into her.

That would've happened if I'd continued to let my emotions rule my body. Yet, as I was emptying her bottle of vodka, I decided to take the rational path instead. The one that led me out of the apartment and into Matthew's office. I swear, the man is half-vampire with the amount of sleep he gets every night.

"I want another job."

*One where I'm not forced to observe her every move.*

Looking up from his computer, he says, entirely unfazed, "You could help out with the Calvetti case." As if he's had a backup plan for this scenario all along.

"Isn't Vance dealing with it already?"

"It's more complex than we thought. He needs all the help he can get."

A challenge, the kind that my rational brain likes. A lot.

"I'll do it."

Matthew nods before he continues, "I'll inform Mason and Jaden that they'll be escorting Lauren to the hospital tomorrow."

"What? Why?"

"Mason arranged a checkup for her. Said you were worried about her."

*Right.*

"Ask the doctor to come here." Just like her therapist, who has been making house calls.

"Since it's been quite a while and she was in a car accident, they want to do a thorough checkup. She has to go there."

I trust Mason with my life and hers. And I know that Jaden, who is one of Matthew's youngest yet highly trained operatives, can keep her safe.

But the thought of her leaving this building, knowing she's dead set on bolting while there's still a significant threat out there, makes my stomach tighten in knots.

"I'll join them."

*Yeah, my rational mind can take a hike because I'm not done. Not yet.*

# Chapter 19
## LAUREN

It's official. I hate hospitals.

Is it the antiseptic smell hitting my nostrils, making me slightly nauseous? Or the bright lights hanging from the ceiling, chasing away all the coziness?

Or maybe it's just the fact that I'm boxed in between Mason and a guy who introduced himself as Jaden—a tall guy with blond-brown wavy hair and a tattoo slithering down one arm—while the one I refuse to acknowledge is sitting right in front of me.

All three of them have joined me at this private clinic.

*Excessive much?*

Yet I've kept my complaints to myself, hoping that I'm here to get back a slice of freedom.

Ironic really, how it was only a week ago when I felt comfortable with being stuck in my room, surrounded by four walls. But now, being cooped up inside feels more like a straitjacket, tightening every minute I'm there.

I had to talk to them.

Make them see that, by keeping me inside, I'd be dead already.

So, I talked to the only person reasonable enough to listen.

*"I want to go for a run." Not giving Mason any time to respond, I added a very important detail, "Outside."*

*"You're not ready yet."* His blue eyes were determined, warning me to drop the subject. With him *not around, Mason was less playful.*

*"You're not a doctor."*

*"I'm not,"* he admitted, hesitating, before he continued, *"We'll ask him this afternoon when we go for your checkup."*

The checkup I almost forgot about. And, now that I'm sitting here, I'm afraid the doctor will say the exact same thing Mason said.

"Liam Ressler," a doctor announces.

*Glad that he could use my appointment to get one himself.*

"We don't like to use your name in public," Mason whispers as he taps my thigh two times, motioning for me to go ahead.

*In public?*

I check the waiting room one more time, confirming that we're alone, before I follow the doctor into his office.

"Everything looks good, Miss—" The doctor stops mid-sentence, waiting for me to fill in the blank.

"Miss Ressler," *he* says before I can open my mouth.

I'm seconds away from claiming we're not related in *any* way, but instead, I bite my lip, focusing on what the doctor has to say.

"Miss Ressler, you passed your physical examination, and your blood results look normal. Now, I was informed that you would like to start running again. Exercise is good, but I would strongly recommend you start off slow, doing mild exercises like swimming, walking, or cycling."

*Is he serious? He couldn't pick a more exciting sport? One where you get to sweat like hell. Where you give everything you've got until you're so exhausted that you end up slouched on a couch or in bed the second you lie down.*

"If you're able to do those activities without any headaches or other pain during and after, you can start jogging again."

*Jogging. I'm no jogger. If I run, I run like hell.*

The doctor looks at me, awaiting my answer on how I'm going to tackle this. Walking is outside, and it's also the closest form to running.

A grin slowly spreads across my lips at the thought of me sprinting off on our walk. Looking up, I see how Mason and *him* take notice, both frowning.

*Damn.*

"I'll start off walking since we don't have a swimming pool," I say, trying to sound less happy.

"We have a swimming pool. It's not a problem," *he* interjects.

"We do?" I ask.

Everyone nods.

A freaking pool in the building.

I won't even have the joy of getting there by car.

# CHAPTER 20
## LAUREN

Swimming—it's not my thing, but if it gets me out of my room, then I'll make it mine. Or, at least, I'm trying, doing a solid rhythm and going up and down at a fast pace until I have to break it off, taking my turn against the wall, reminding me again why I hate it so much.

Even though this pool is as big as the average public pool with a stunning view of the city of New York, it's too small. There's just no pool that could swallow all my grief. That's why I love running—no limitations, no walls, no forced breaks.

Yet I plunged into the pool, knowing it was the only option if I wanted to exhaust my body.

So focused on perfecting my front crawl, it takes me a while to figure out that a certain sound is in fact someone yelling my name.

Someone who thinks I need a lifeguard to go for a swim.

Someone who assumes he has the right to disturb my workout.

Someone who I ignore. Or, well, I try, as he's quite persistent, ruining my exercise session, which forces me to stop in the middle of the pool.

My eyes zone in on a very pissed off male dressed in a dark blue shirt and a pair of jeans, standing along the side of the pool.

He composes himself a little before he commands, "Get out of the pool. You've had enough."

"Says who?" the child inside me asks.

"Start off slow. Doctor's orders," he refutes, giving me an excruciating glare.

"This is me starting slow."

*Well, not quite. But I could go faster, so it's not entirely a lie.*

"You've been swimming nonstop for a whole hour. You're done."

Swimming is supposed to relieve stress. Instead, he's making it worse. If he keeps this up, I'll leave the pool with even more frustrations than I had when I jumped in. I have to negotiate before this workout ends up being entirely useless.

"Give me another fifteen minutes."

*If I step it up a little, I might be able to work with that.*

"I'll give you fifteen seconds." His jaw clenches and unclenches as he takes a step closer to the edge of the pool.

I have no clue how far he's willing to go. I'm practically in the middle of the pool, and he's fully clothed on the side.

With the water as a barrier, I decide to take my chances and do a few more laps. Besides, I would love to see him jump into the pool with his clothes on.

Vigorously kicking my legs while I swing one arm at a time up and past my shoulder, I get brief flashes of my surroundings every time I lift my head out of the water to take a deep breath. Still, it's enough to track his movement to the other side of the pool, to the spot where I'm heading.

I'll be damned if I let him get to me, so I give up my turn against the wall, and I start floating on my back in the other direction, eyes on him.

And what a fun game this is, almost more exciting than swimming my ass off. But that's only my opinion. He clearly doesn't agree as he gives me another murderous glare before he halts along the border of the pool, grasping the bottom of his shirt before pulling it over his head, revealing his ripped body.

*Even though he's a douche, he sure has a nice package.*

Stripping down his pants, he dives into the water, wearing boxers only.

And the only thing I'm doing is floating.

In the same spot.

Where he's heading to.

*No. No. No.*

Turning around, I start swimming in the opposite direction. Kicking my legs harder, I give it everything I've got, which isn't a lot when I've been swimming for over sixty minutes. And, to make things even worse, I get a major cramp in both my legs.

*Damn.*

Excruciating pain shoots through my calves, a cramp I've had before, one I know exactly how to fix as I reach out for my toes, tugging on them.

Being in a swimming pool does make the whole technique a bit more challenging since I'm underwater, unable to breathe. Letting go of my toes, I try to make my way back to the surface to take a much-needed breath when an arm snakes around my upper body, pulling me upward.

*What the hell?*

The minute my head's above the water, I gasp while my cramp still urges me to pull my toes. But *his* tight rescue hold prevents me from doing that. He just drags me along to the edge of the pool where he turns me around, hands on my hips, as he's about to lift me out of the water.

*No way.*

Leaning against the wall, I brush off his hands. "I can get out myself," I lie while I push up on my toes to tackle the ongoing muscle cramp.

"You almost fucking drowned, and that's what you want to argue about?" he fumes, his eyes pinning me to the spot while his arms are now holding the wall on either side of me, caging me in.

"I wasn't drowning! I was stretching my legs underwater," I explain.

"Fine, let's see it then. Go on and get out of the water." He motions with his hand. He's not touching me, but if I were to go down, his arms would prevent me from slipping beneath the water.

"You need to get out first."

"You're full of shit, Lauren," he hisses, inching closer, his chest almost pressing against mine.

I avoid his eyes by looking down, and I get an up-close view of his toned body pressed up against my red bikini.

His face mere inches from mine, he presses his knee between my thighs before he demands, "What the hell happened?"

*You mean, what the hell is happening?*

The only thing I do know is, whatever *this* is, it has to stop.

Placing my hands on the edge of the pool, I lift myself out of the water, my body brushing against his chest in the process, before I walk off.

My legs fully cooperate.

My values are perfectly intact.

Only my body seems to malfunction.

As it's still buzzing in the aftermath of his proximity.

# CHAPTER 21
## LAUREN

Soaking in the bathtub, I'm surrounded by foam as I try to ease the tension out of my body without exhausting it.

"Gorgeous?" Mason's muffled voice sounds through the door.

My blissful peace is disturbed as he urgently knocks two times, my eyes set on the door I locked firmly.

"What are you doing?"

*Isn't it obvious?*

Although I have to admit, it is a bit unusual for me to be locked inside the bathroom for so long since they had to encourage me every few days to take a shower for the past few months.

"Open this goddamn door!" another male voice rumbles.

*Look who decided to join the party.*

Pressing my lips together, I refuse to say anything. And, to make sure of that, I close my eyes before I let my body slip beneath the foam-covered water.

As I'm being surrounded by nothingness, the background noises are drowned out. That is, until a loud bang forces me to resurface and acknowledge that the door is no longer in its rightful place.

*Nope.*

It's slammed against the wall while *he* fills up the empty space.

"What the hell are you doing?" he roars before he approaches, as if my head isn't enough of an indication that I'm in the freaking tub.

"What does it look like I'm doing?" I shout back as I motion to myself—my very naked self—who is very grateful now for pouring too much bath foam product into the tub. There's still enough foam left to cover up the most delicate parts of my body.

"You were drowning in the pool only an hour ago, and now, you're in the tub!" he states. "Get out!"

People who get under my skin the way he does are very much extinct. I have no clue how to handle him. I can only reach out to the one person who knows him best.

I set eyes on Mason, who's lingering by the door. "Is *he* serious?"

The only response I get is a small shoulder shrug.

"Two minutes to get out; that's it," *he* barks as he turns around, yanking a white towel off a rack before throwing it at me.

I can barely catch it, much less hold it above the water, but he doesn't care. He turns around and motions for Mason to leave the room before he does.

I grunt.

*Two minutes?*

I don't need that much time to rise out of the water, wrap the small towel around my body, and march my butt out of the bathroom and toward the living room. Moving around confirms the tininess of the towel, which barely covers my body in a decent way, but I have no time for such *small* details.

*No.*

All my attention goes out to the guy who's been on a collision course with me since the day he laid eyes on me. The guy who just crossed a line, erased it, and redrew it in a place that is simply too close to home.

I need to set my boundaries.

I need to make my demands.

I need to make him see that Lauren Miller isn't somebody you can order around.

As I head straight for him, I pass by Mason and Jaden—my audience for what probably will be quite a show—but my body is a ticking time bomb with only one mission—to reach the target before it goes off.

I'm even able to approach him without him noticing since he's got his back to me. Only when I'm in touching distance does he turn around to face me.

"What the hell is your problem?" I shriek as I place my hands on his black shirt. Surprised by my own strength, I manage to make him sway while I pray I'm still a master at securing a towel nice and snug below my armpits.

Except for the small waver, he keeps still, his mouth a tight line as he scours every inch of my body, disregarding my question, until his dark eyes meet mine again, blazing with a fierce intensity.

I must say, his tension is contagious because, whenever he's around, I feel the same way.

"I've had enough of you! Enough of your temper! Enough of you bossing me around! You're not my family, you're not my friend, you're not my anything!"

I shove him again, but this time, he doesn't budge, not a freaking inch, his body solid in place.

He briefly averts his eyes to the left before he sets them back on me, proving his eyes really can get a hell of a lot darker than the chocolate brown a lot of girls probably swoon for.

The eyes that have me very much distracted, as he's able to catch me off guard when he grabs on to my arm, dragging me after him through the hallway.

I resist. I make every effort not to follow his lead, but his steel grip is so firm; I can only stumble after him as I hold on to my towel for dear life.

He pulls me into my bedroom and slams the door behind himself before turning to face me, the definition of enraged right in front of me.

"You want to talk? Then, talk, but don't you ever walk like that in front of another guy again!" he exclaims, gesturing to my towel, which is still firmly in place.

Since he's still close to the door with enough distance between us, I feel brave enough to speak up. "I'll wear whatever the hell I want, where I want, when I want! You know why? Because this"—I gesture to my body—"is my body, and you have nothing to say about it!"

His eyes flash with a fierceness that makes me regret my spunk.

"You haven't changed one bit!" he says in a low, quiet voice as he approaches me like a predator, ready to eat me—not because he's hungry, just because he can.

Seeing his jaw is set, his hands balled into fists, I know he can.

So, I do the only reasonable thing. I shuffle backward, but three steps later, my back hits a wall.

Instead of figuring a way out, I take the time to silently curse my parents for not giving me the height to stand up against him.

"I'm really starting to question if you have a brain in that head of yours. Because you sure as hell ain't using it!" he booms. Taking the final step, he's less than a foot away from me now.

Focusing on his words and not the closeness of his body, I rise to my full height as I lash out with courage I only get when someone threatens to get too close. "Are you calling me stupid?"

"Do not twist my words, Lauren! You're done with my behavior? Well, I'm definitely done with yours! You need to stop being a bitch, stop flirting your way through life, and stop running away from your problems," he booms as he slams his hands against the wall.

His words detonate something inside me that makes me careless of the fact that I don't have enough inches to overwhelm him or enough muscle power to make him feel fragile and small. This feeling tears through my veins, urging my body into doing the one thing my mind knows won't work. Just like a reflex, my conscience has no say in the matter; it can only brace for the outcome as my hand lashes out.

Catching my hand midair, his eyes boring into mine, he threatens, "Don't."

Unimpressed by his reflexes, I glare, my body glowing beneath his touch while my mind refuses to submit, suggesting a maneuver that'll make him crumble to the ground. I just need to move a little to the side, so I can lift my knee.

This time, my mind and body work together as a team.

My movement is quick.

My aim accurate.

Yet, in a flash, I'm on the floor with him on top.

As our positions have drastically switched, so have our moods.

When I connect with his dark brown eyes, a warm flood engulfs me, my body hyperaware in a whole different way.

With the hold of his left hand on my upper arm, his right arm pressing into my back, his fingers digging into the side of my hip, I realize that, for the first time, it feels like an embrace instead of a restraint.

"What are you doing to me, Lauren?" he asks.

With his head sagging forward, his forehead touching mine, I see a glimpse of what I think is sorrow shining through his rage.

Yet I could ask him the very same thing.

It's beyond my comprehension how, in the blink of an eye, he can obliterate every hateful thing he's ever said or done.

Squeezing my eyes closed, I try not to think about his body on top of mine. Or his warm breath prickling my skin.

Until the pressure of his body is gone.

All that's left is coldness, followed by a hard slam of a closing door.

I'm not surprised.

I'm not hurt.

He's like air to me—invisible, worthless.

If only my body didn't need it to survive.

# CHAPTER 22
## LAUREN

He's *gone.*

Only five days before Christmas, and he has disappeared.

*I don't care.*

In fact, I hate the holidays. It's for families, for happy people like Sarah, who breathe the Christmas spirit. I'd skip the holidays in a heartbeat.

"He'll come back," Sarah explains, hanging another red Christmas ball on the enormous tree she insisted on having in Mason's living room.

"Who?" I play dumb as I'm lying on the couch, watching *Game of Thrones* on HBO.

"You know who. His sister called because she couldn't find someone to pick her up from the airport; that's why he didn't have the time to say good-bye."

*Perfect. Who needs him anyway when you have Jon Snow to keep you company?*

"Catherine just came home from a trip to Europe after getting out of rehab. Knowing Liam, he'll probably hover a bit during the holidays."

*Sounds like I should send Catherine a thank-you card for taking over my role.*

"You know, Greg would love to celebrate Christmas Eve or New Year's Eve with—"

"No!" I yell, eyes set on her, making my answer as clear as daylight. "I don't want to see him," I breathe, my fingers digging into the fabric of the couch as I battle a swarm of memories I've caught and hidden as well as I can.

"Sorry, Lauren, I didn't want to upset you."

"I'm not upset." I sigh away my own lie. "I just don't want any visitors."

"I'll tell Matthew."

Her facial expression is enough of an indication that I'll never be able to hold him off forever. But, for now, I'm safe.

My only objective is suffering through the next two weeks. I can only hope there'll be enough eggnog to wash away the holiday spirit.

# Chapter 23
## LIAM

*I left.*

Catherine's homecoming couldn't have had better timing, giving me permission to leave the way I did—getting in my Audi and driving away without so much as a good-bye.

Lying on top of her, feeling every curve of her body pressed against mine, I forgot for a second what I was doing.

But then my eyes fell on her right temple, which is now marred by a scar.

A reminder of my failure.

A warning for me to not get emotionally involved.

I had to leave.

If only to find my sanity, prevent myself from hurting her more than the words coming out of my mouth. I refuse to add more scars to her body because I'm not focused enough to protect her.

And, even though I've called Mason and Matthew one too many times, I've managed to stay away, focusing my attention on my sister, who's finally growing into the woman I've always known was hidden inside her.

Although she's still headstrong, fighting off my well-intended brotherly advice, I'm less bothered about it, knowing her body isn't guided by filthy drugs.

"Liam, your phone is ringing."

Coming out of the kitchen with two cans of soda and a plate of nachos, I stride toward the coffee table, putting it all down before I grab my phone.

*Mason calling.*

My pulse kicking up while my mouth dries out. "What happened?"

Catherine throws me a worried look at the sound of my voice, one she knows all too well. I haven't really told her much—well, absolutely nothing—about what's been going on.

"Relax, Liam. She's fine."

I exhale, smothering my popped-up worries. "What is it, Mase?"

"I should've asked yesterday when I called—"

Walking up to the window, I press, "Out with it."

"Sebastian's birthday—it's the day after tomorrow, and we're all going out to celebrate it."

Sebastian used to work side by side with Matthew in the field. Now, he's Matthew's right-hand man for the Critical Response Department and a close friend.

"I was just wondering if you wanted to tag along."

"You're all going out," I repeat, letting his message sink in when I start to realize why he's been dreading this call. Turning around, I head in the direction of my bedroom, ignoring my sister's furrowed eyebrows as I pass her. "She can't go out."

"We're going to The Qbe, and we're using the VIP room. It's fine. Matthew and Quinn are handling it."

Quinn is the owner of The Qbe and a reliable friend of Matthew. We tend to celebrate birthdays of team and family members at The Qbe, although we mostly don't use the VIP room.

"Besides, we could all use some good time out of this building. We can't keep her locked up forever."

There's no hesitation when I answer, "Yes, we can."

"You haven't been around. She's been doing her best. But, shit, man, even she has the right to go out." He pauses. "Anyway, I wasn't calling for permission. I just wanted to know if I should add you to the guest list or not," he finishes, sounding irritated.

Even though every cell in my body is screaming to go back, I can't just up and leave Catherine. "I'll think about it."

We say our good-byes right before I walk back to my sister, whose face is covered in question marks.

"Who's the girl you're fussing over?"

Even if I wasn't dreading her sisterly opinion on the topic, I wouldn't want her to get involved. It's too dangerous. The less she knows, the better.

"There is no girl, Cat."

"Right, William," she snaps sarcastically, using my full name that she knows I hate. "I've loved having you around for the holidays, but I'm twenty-one years old. You can't stay forever. I know you're working for SPISe now."

"I'm taking some time off."

"You've taken two weeks off already! Besides, Phoebe is looking for a place to stay."

Phoebe is Cat's best friend—and the only decent friend I trust—who joined her on her trip to Europe.

"If you don't mind her staying here, she can move in. I won't be alone. I'll even come visit you—"

"Let's watch the movie, shall we?"

"Fuck, William, you're stubborn."

*Yeah, I am.*

That's why I press play and ignore my persistent sister.

Until a half hour later when she informs me out of the blue, "Phoebe's moving in with me. You have to move out," with her phone in hand and a smile on her face.

"You're evicting me out of my *own* apartment?" I confirm as I stare at her, dumbfounded.

Yet her demand isn't what bothers me; it's the fact that, with the little information she got earlier, she's taking the decision to leave out of my hands.

Shaking my head, I press play, not discussing it any further. That is, until we've finished the movie, and I've made up my own mind.

Texting Mason, I realize there's really only one option.

I'll be there.

# Chapter 24
## Lauren

My semi-transparent white shirt hangs loosely over my stomach, and my tight jeans hug my legs in all the right places. A layer of fabric enforces my defenses, giving me much-needed strength that I haven't had in a long time.

Embracing this long-lost feeling, I survey my reflection in the bathroom mirror, and I see the new and improved Lauren, who has kept her prying fingers away from the elevator keypad, her insanity in check, and her grief nicely stashed away. Because of her, I get to go out and celebrate Sebastian's birthday, a guy I barely know but am totally grateful for.

Dragging in a deep breath, I slip into a blue sweater before I make my way to the living room.

"You look great," Sarah acknowledges as she jumps up from the couch, the rim of her pink skirt flailing as she walks up to me. Her arms going around my body, she hugs me so tight; I'm sure she's trying to squeeze the darkness right out of me.

Although I'm still getting used to her closeness, it's hard to stay unaffected, especially after we've been spending a lot of time together, celebrating Christmas and New Year's Eve. It would've all been unbearable without her.

"You girls ready?" Mason asks as he enters the living room in dark jeans, a white shirt that is unbuttoned on top, a deep blue jacket, and no baseball cap to hide his disheveled light-brown hair.

"Yes, we are!" Sarah answers, self-assured, as she lets go of me.

"Could you leave us alone for a moment?" Mason asks Sarah while I take in his casual-chic style.

"Sure. I'll go and get Matthew."

"Tell him we're ready to leave," Mason adds right before Sarah disappears into the elevator. He turns around, looking my body up and down.

It's been a while since I've let my hair down or worn fashionable clothes fulfilling more than just its primary purpose.

"Gorgeous," he states, his tone of voice different than usual.

I've been around enough these past few months to know that, when he starts raking his hand through his hair, something's definitely up.

"What is it?"

"Liam isn't happy about this."

Looking up at him, I'm sure my mouth is hanging wide open. "What?"

"I talked to him. Actually, it took some convincing from all of us, but he agreed."

*Agreed? He hasn't been around for over two weeks. What the hell gives him the right to even have a say in the matter?*

"I assured Liam that nothing would happen, that you needed this." His hand rakes once more through his hair. "Don't make me regret it. Don't do anything foolish tonight, like run off alone, not even for a toilet break," he finishes, sounding a little out of breath.

As much as I want to focus on *him* and his overbearing attitude, I set my eyes on Mason, the everlasting knight in shining armor, the first guy who made it on my decent-guy list, who never limits my swimming sessions to one hour or my time in bed to ten hours, who never crowds me in a way *he* would. And, apparently, the guy who fought with his own friend to give me this one night out.

It's enough reason for me to nod, assuring him that I'll be on my best behavior.

Taking a step closer, Mason kisses the top of my head before he steps back, a smile tugging at his lips while a load of stress seems to run down his shoulders.

Too stunned to do something, much less say anything, he breaks the silence by stating, "Let's get this show on the road." He strolls to the elevator, pushing in the code. "Oh, and no alcohol for you tonight. You're not twenty-one yet."

Coming to stand next to him, I explain, "I don't need alcohol to have fun." I *never* drink to have fun. I drink to forget.


We meet up with Matthew and Sarah on the company floor before we all pile into the elevator, riding to the basement of the building. Matthew is wearing a pair of jeans, which perfectly fits his more relaxed mood.

While Matthew is holding Sarah close to his side, Mason and I keep a safe distance. That is, until the elevator doors open up to the basement floor, and he's right by my side.

I stare at the two black Range Rovers lined up fifteen feet away from us.

"We'll see each other in a bit," Sarah whispers, squeezing my hand before she and Matthew walk up to the first car.

"We're taking that one." Mason motions to the second car. "Matthew likes to drive himself," he explains further while he places his hand on my lower back, guiding me to the right car.

I follow his lead until something in the corner of my eye catches my attention.

As if my feet are suddenly glued to the concrete floor, I halt.

Hyperaware of my surroundings.

Hyperaware of *him.*

While the coldness of the basement cools down my exposed skin, I can't seem to contain the fire blazing inside me.

Leaning against a black Ducati, feet crossed at the ankles, he's wearing black leather pants and a matching leather vest while holding a helmet in his right hand. His thick, disheveled hair keeps my eyes away from his dark and dangerous scowl.

For a split second, my treacherous body forgets the fact that he just left me for two freaking weeks.

Not a word.

No phone call.

No visit.

No nothing.

"Let's get you in the car," Mason says, his hand touching my lower back, reminding me that I'm still standing frozen to the spot.

My breathing nowhere near normal, I pivot around and let Mason guide me up to the car. He opens the back door for me to get in before he slides in right after.

"Lauren, this is Bryan." Mason points out the broad-shouldered man—his handsome face marred by a faint scar above his left eyebrow—sitting behind the wheel, who gives me a curt nod. "And you remember Jaden."

The guy who saw me in nothing but a towel.

*How could I not remember him?*

"They're joining us tonight."

I get what he's saying, but I'm not going to focus on the security measures they're taking. Instead, I gaze out the dark tinted window to see how *he* gets on his sleek black bike, helmet on, eyes set on the exit before he races out of the parking lot.

*Didn't expect anything else.*

But I'm glad. With Mason not being his usual self and the two guys up front in full work mode, the mood in the car is already way above stress level.

Fifteen minutes later, we're still driving. The atmosphere in the car has shifted from uncomfortable to unbearable. I'm seconds away from getting out of a moving car when it slows down, a nightclub coming into view. We approach the entrance of the building, but then we drive right past it, and I shoot a questioning look at Mason.

"Back door," he utters.

We drive into a small alley, parking right behind Matthew and Sarah's car—who we lost track of along the way—and next to a Ducati.

Looking to my right, at the back door of the club, which is as close as you can park a car without scratching its shiny surface, I see Matthew, Sarah, a bouncer holding open the door, and the guy who *really* shouldn't be here, waiting.

*No. Freaking. Way.*

Jaden, who just got out, opens the back door at Mason's side.

"Follow me," Mason says, giving me a glance before he gets out.

As hard as it is to move in *his* direction, I slide over the leather backseat, my body coiling with tension. I almost fall over when my right foot touches the ground. I'm truly grateful that Mason is in full work mode, as his arm prevents me from embarrassing myself.

"Careful," he whispers, my side pressing against his hip while his arm remains in place.

About to push some distance in between us, I notice a shadow approaching.

I don't need to take a look to confirm what my body already knows. Mason's closeness might not be so bad.

Looking up at him, I say, "Let's go."

Since Mason is as eager as I am to get inside, I manage to avoid *him* when we follow the bouncer through a narrow hallway inside the club.

"We have to pass the restrooms in the main hall," the bouncer explains as we approach a hallway, a few people in sight.

Mason grabs my hand, squeezing it two times. "Stick close."

I try really hard to ignore the anxious vibe he's broadcasting when we near the first stranger. Then, *he*, who should've driven his bike across the country, suddenly appears on the other side of me, forming a barrier between me and anyone who might pass me on my right side.

Sandwiched in between Mason and *him*, I try to ignore every brush of his arm against mine and every belly flutter that comes with it as we make it to the VIP room.

The bouncer guides us along a purple-and-blue-illuminated dance floor, located in the middle of the room, to a private lounge area in the corner of the room, which has several white leather couches and a modern, large—and, of course, white—coffee table.

Plopping down on one of the couches, I look up to see how *he* walks off.

The view of his back is becoming all too familiar.

The headache that comes with it is a nasty habit.

Luckily, I know the perfect medicine for that.

"I want to dance," I announce, jumping up.

Mason's body blocks my way to the dance floor. "We'll dance. Don't worry. But, first, let's just sit down and drink something." He motions to the couch before he rakes a hand through his hair.

I had high hopes for this evening, but they're crumbling with every passing second.

I didn't expect it to be like *this.*

"Lauren?" Mason stresses, still facing me, seconds away from dumping my ass on the couch.

*Right. Sitting down.*

The lounge area is quite big, and I spot Sarah across from us, already cooped up on another couch with Matthew standing next to her, talking to the bouncer who guided us here. I take a step toward her when Mason gets in my way.

"Where are you going?"

*Breathe, Lauren.*

"I'm going to sit with Sarah." I point to the only person in this room who's normal. "Please." I force the word out of my mouth as if it were poison. I normally don't beg. Ever. But, right now, I'm desperate.

"Fine." He relents, a little angry.

*Dear Lord.*

All the couches are so close to each other that I can't even move my arm without him noticing. He's got nothing to worry about.

Walking toward Sarah, I plop down next to her on the couch while Matthew and the bouncer walk off.

"So glad you're here! One more second near them, and I'd have lost it for sure." I sigh.

"You get used to it," she answers, knowing exactly what I'm talking about. "I don't mind."

A little astonished by her answer, a "What?" escapes my mouth.

Mason and Jaden, sitting to the side from us, scrutinize me, as if I'd just committed a major crime.

*This is going to be a long night.*

I give them my best, sincerest fake smile before I shift my attention back to Sarah.

"It's like this all the time?" I whisper-hiss.

"Matthew is always tense when we go out. I guess it's a job thing. But they're normally not *this* stressed. You're special," she explains as if that were a good thing.

"Special treatment for me. Yay," I cheer sarcastically.

"They care about you. And they're all good at their jobs because they're always anticipating the worst."

"At the cost of being like *that* nonstop?" I point at them in the smallest movement I can possibly make, which they still notice. "I'll let them settle down, but I definitely want to dance. I won't wait forever."

"You're gonna dance?" she asks, a little unsure.

"Of course! You will, too, right?"

"I don't dance."

"You do!"

"At home." She sighs. "I can't do that here."

"Yes, you can. I refuse to dance without you!"

And I know exactly what can help her as I shift my gaze to a waiter passing by. "Excuse me," I interrupt as I slightly lift my body off the seat to get the waiter's attention. I notice both Jaden and Mason getting up. Holding out my hand, palm up, I manage to stop them from moving over as I sit back down before I make my order. "A strawberry daiquiri, please." Mason's eyes flash with warning, but I continue, "For this lovely lady here." I point in Sarah's direction.

"You want to have a cocktail, Sarah?" Mason asks, moving over to a couch nearby.

Afraid that Sarah will back down because of him, I answer, "Yes, she wants one. Why is that a problem?"

"Don't force her to drink alcohol," he warns.

I'm a little stunned at his accusation.

"Why would you think that?" I snap back.

"Because she usually doesn't drink."

"You've never tasted a strawberry daiquiri?" I ask, dumbfounded, my eyes shifting from Mason to Sarah.

She shrugs, confirming she hasn't tried it before.

*Freaking hell.*

"You want to try one?" I whisper only for her to hear.

"I don't know. I don't think Matthew approves."

Now, I really need to order one.

"She wants one," I state firmly. "She can take a sip, and you can finish the rest," I suggest, pointing a finger at Mason, whose scowl only lessens a tiny bit.

*Another point for the overprotective, future brother-in-law.*

He clearly doesn't know I would never let her get too drunk. Not like last time. Yet I feel I should expose her to new things, as it's pretty obvious that the Scott brothers only do the opposite.

Sarah is a grown woman, about two years older than me. The girl can have a freaking daiquiri.

"Earth to Lauren," Sarah sings, waving her hand in front of my face.

"What did you say?"

"What do you want to drink?" Sarah asks, pointing at the waiter, who's still waiting.

"I'll have a cocktail," I say, followed by another vicious look from Mason, who's about to correct me. "A nonalcoholic one," I add with a big smile.

An hour later, and our party crowd has expanded. Jaden; Sebastian, the birthday boy; Bryan; and two other men who introduced themselves as Colin, a sturdy man with a deep-set of dark eyes, and Dean, a dark-skinned man with hair buzzed close to the skull, have joined us. Matthew and Jaden even had to add another couch, which boxes us in.

Coincidence or not? *Yeah, I don't think so.*

I've finished about three nonalcoholic cocktails while Sarah drank two daiquiris and a water. She liked it, but just like last time, it was enough for her to transform into an overly happy-wasted kind of state. Hopefully, she's still capable of dancing.

But first ...

"I need to go to the restroom," I say loud enough for everyone to hear. It's not really in my nature to ask permission. And, since *he* hasn't been around, I want to go now.

"Let's go." Mason, who received my message, motions for me to follow him. He comes to stand next to me, Jaden following suit.

"I need to go, too," Sarah whines, frantically looking around, probably in search of Matthew, who hasn't been around much either.

I take her by the arm and ignore the fact that she's searching for Matthew to go take a pee.

"Come with us. The more, the merrier." I smile resentfully as I glance at both Mason and Jaden.

I've been to parties where I almost couldn't turn my head without my drink being spiked, but now, we're in a freaking VIP lounge, and they're still like this. Shaking my head, I turn around and hold on to Sarah while I follow the restroom signs.

We're about ten feet away from the restroom when Mason stops us from entering while Jaden walks in.

*Hello? Toilet for women!*

"All clear," Jaden affirms, coming back out.

*Seriously?*

Mason told me I couldn't go to the toilet alone, but to push it to this level is beyond my comprehension.

"Are you sure? Don't you need another look?"

As they're both pretty close, they glare down at me.

"Come on, Lauren. I really need to go," Sarah pleads.

They can thank her later. I follow her into the restroom where Sarah disappears into a stall while I take another one.

"You ready to dance?" I ask Sarah when I'm washing my hands.

"Absolutely." Only an hour ago, it was a simple no.

We exit the restroom where Mason and Jaden are still waiting. Yet, now, there are two women behind them.

"About time," one of the women chimes.

And then I notice they're not just standing there, hanging around; Jaden is holding them back.

"You could've let them in. I can handle myself around women," I inform Mason. *Heck, I can handle myself around men. Those two wouldn't have been a problem at all.*

"And, now, the queen is going to have a talk," the same woman complains to her friend.

She gets my full attention.

"Are you talking to me?"

In a flash, the mood in the hallway changes from casual to tense. Mason tries to use his body as a barrier when I slip to his side.

"I wasn't, but now that I am, move your fat ass, so we can pass," she says.

*If you thought that VIP bitches didn't exist, well, think again.*

I make a move forward, but Mason's arm pushes me back.

"Don't."

He can't stop me, yet Sarah can. Her subtle touch on my shoulder is the only reason I let this slide.

Grabbing ahold of her hand, I walk away with only one thing on my mind. "Let's dance."

As I hold Sarah's hand above her head, she's got one leg off the ground while she pushes up to her toes with her other leg before she whirls around.

I keep her balanced, letting her practice her pirouette. It's absolutely silly, not at all like I would dance with Amy. Yet, for once, it isn't about anyone but us, having fun regardless of what anyone might think. Even though Jaden and Mason are near, they keep a distance, giving us enough space for us to practice our ballet moves.

That is, until three songs later, when Matthew swoops in, hands planted on Sarah's waist while he says something in her ear.

Although she was happy when we were dancing, I can see the difference now that she's in Matthew's arms. How she warms to his touch, how she's more at ease with him by her side—something I could never imagine having with a guy, yet somehow, it fits them.

With the dance floor getting a lot more crowded and the DJ playing upbeat music, I have no problem with dancing alone.

"Let's take a break," Mason yells in my ear when the crowd keeps thickening.

His gaze flits around the room, his anxiousness evident.

I know he's got reasons. The guy behind me has been subtly touching me every now and then without Jaden and Mason noticing. At first, I thought it was accidental, but now, I'm sure he's trying to weasel his way closer. If he keeps this up, there'll be at least five guys ready to pummel him to the ground.

Instead of letting them handle my problems, I'd rather solve them myself. Or I am about to, but the asshat is gaining confidence real fast, his hands on my hips, trying to make me swing along with him. A bold move, one that doesn't go unnoticed by Mason, who's pulling me toward him, seconds away from giving this dude a night he won't forget.

A night I won't forget either.

One that ends with me in the corner of our lounge area, surrounded by all of them—or worse, in a car back to SPISe, only to never get out of that building again.

*No way.*

My hand on Mason's shirt, I keep him from moving forward, shaking my head, as it's my turn to warn him off. "Don't."

Yet Mason refuses to acknowledge me, fixated on the dude behind me, who doesn't mind a little competition.

There's only one scenario left where I can physically hold Mason back while I send a clear message to the guy behind me.

One I wouldn't even consider if it wasn't for *him*, who I spot across the room.

His eyes burn with a promise.

He's on the verge of committing murder.

Eyes set on his victim.

Mason.

The only guy in *his* line of vision, who's holding me close, so *he's* oblivious to the threat behind me.

Even though my conscience cringes at the thought of using this situation, I can't let this opportunity slide. I can't let it go that *he* hasn't been around tonight, that he hasn't been around for two freaking weeks.

Now that I'm finally having a good time, he's back.

*Game on.*

Closing the distance between Mason and me, I slide my hand over his shoulder while I pull him flush against my body.

It's a strange feeling, and since Mason is looking at me, completely horrified, I know that he feels the same way.

"What are you doing?" he yells above the music, his eyes following my gaze, looking over his shoulder to where *he's* at.

If it wasn't for Bryan holding *him* back, he'd already be snapping Mason's neck.

"Getting rid of that asshole behind me," I answer, my head next to his.

Mason looks back at me. "He's the least of our problems."

He's absolutely right, yet I'm all fired up, unstoppable. I'm ready to cross a line, a major one, but my mind is set on getting what it wants.

*Revenge.*

Mason doesn't see it coming. And I barely realize what I'm doing until my head inches closer, and I slam my lips against his.

Even though Mason is a very handsome guy and probably an awesome kisser, it feels awkward as hell, like I'm kissing my own brother, making me entirely grateful when our kiss gets interrupted.

As swiftly as I placed my mouth on Mason's lips, I am being pulled out of his arms, picked up, and tossed over someone's shoulder. Someone with a lot of muscles and a high pace, as I bounce with every step he takes.

There's really only one person who would have such a hard time with me kissing Mason.

Really only one guy who would react in such a bold way.

*Him.*

As I start to kick and scream, the hold on me only tightens, making it hard for me to fight and breathe at the same time.

"What are you doing, Liam?" someone yells. "Put her down," the same voice suggests from nearby as we go through a dark hallway.

Still upside down, my hair semi-obscuring my view, I notice we're being followed by a guy I haven't seen before, and Matthew.

"Stay out of it, Max," *he* snaps to the unknown guy.

"Liam," Matthew insists.

*He* ignores them both as we go through a solid door before we exit the building into the cold night.

When we come to a sudden halt, my world spins yet again as my feet hit the ground. Completely out of breath from my struggle and slightly dizzy, I look up at *him,* totally unfazed, as if he didn't just carry one hundred twenty-five pounds over his shoulder from the dance floor to here.

"Bryan can take you both home," Matthew suggests.

I have no vision of Matthew, my eyes set on *his* clenched jaw, his determined eyes.

"Get me two helmets and my jacket."

I wait for Matthew to object, to say something in my defense. But the only thing I hear is the slam of a metal door.

I whip my head around to see a closed door and no Matthew. No Max.

Really, nobody.

All that's left is a dark alley, *his* bike, him, and me—boxed in between his body in front of me and his bike behind me.

"I'll go with Bryan," I suggest.

Still glaring at the door, he says, "No," with a tone that brooks no argument.

No words can get me out of this situation.

No physical moves can get me away from him.

As Matthew returns with two helmets, a pair of black gloves, and a jacket, he says, "Drive safe," and I realize I'm completely screwed.

Leaving me with no other choice but to slide into his jacket before he pushes the helmet over my head.

"Get on," he orders.

*Maybe I can roll myself over this bike and—*

"Don't."

One word cancels my plan.

"Get. On."

Two words I have to digest, a poison I'm forced to take.

I've never ridden on the back of a bike. Heck, I've never been on a bike in general. Driving with him on that death trap of his while he's in full control is out of the question. But that's my opinion, which he couldn't care less about.

I stretch my body to its fullest height while adrenaline surges to every corner of my body.

"If you don't do it, I will," he promises.

It's a promise I know he can execute. He just carried me over his shoulder without so much as one droplet of sweat. I lost this damn fight the moment Matthew and Max left me, forcing me to leave my dignity—or what's left of it—behind in this dark alley and suck it up.

*He'll get my wrath—sooner rather than later.*

Swinging my leg over the bike, I get on, scooting away while he gets on in front of me.

With our bodies completely apart, I hold on to the railing behind me as I realize I could easily jump off without him noticing.

Right when I consider doing exactly that, he revs the engine, gunning it twice. The sound of it is so loud. I don't get the time to run my actions through my brain as I press my body against his, arms squeezing around his waist, before he's off, driving at full speed.

The way he maneuvers his bike through traffic is absolutely horrendous. He's so far gone; he doesn't even consider the possibility of me falling off.

My eyes firmly squeezed closed, I can only cling to him, holding on for dear life, while every minute seems to drag on forever.

Until we finally slow down, driving off the road and into the grass of a secluded area.

Until we come to an abrupt halt, and I immediately jump off regardless of my shaky legs.

Only one thought is in my mind.

*I have to get away from him.*

Striding toward a bunch of nothingness while cars keep on racing by, I pull off the helmet and throw it on the ground, a different tension in my body rising with every step I take as everything replays in my head.

Carrying me out of the club the way he did.

Using my fear to control me.

Risking my life to get rid of his own anger.

All those thoughts invade my mind as I stride away.

No footsteps behind me.

Not a word from him.

Whipping my head around, I see him sitting on his bike, both hands holding the handlebars while the engine is still running, almost as if he's considering leaving me here with no person or building in sight.

Some part of me wishes he would. Then again, I would be stuck here with a pile of anger and nobody to give it to.

My hands balled into fists, I scream, "What the fuck is wrong with you?"

Another minute goes by with him frozen on his bike before he cuts the engine.

"I'm talking to you, *Liam*," I say, spitting out his name for the very first time, as I make my way back to him.

And even then, he takes his time in slowly getting off his bike, peeling off his gloves, seemingly less tense. Driving like a freaking kamikaze pilot did serve its purpose. For him.

"Do you have a death wish?" I hiss.

His indifferent attitude is revving my engine as I march right up to him, daring him to say something, do something, anything. Yet he stays unfazed, his eyes set on the grass between my feet, and I'm almost ready to bolt.

But then I remember the reason that drove him over the edge in the first place.

The trigger that got us here in the first place.

"You've got a problem with me kissing Mason?"

The perfect question to get his attention.

*Freaking hell.*

That's exactly what I see in his defrosted eyes. If eye color could change, I would swear it just got ten shades darker. Yet

I want more. I'm about to describe my kiss in full detail when, in a flash, he pulls me to him and crushes his mouth on mine. Unlike my kiss with Mason, *he* presses his tongue to the seam of my lips, demanding entrance. One I can't seem to deny as he deepens our kiss while I wrap my hands around his neck, letting him pull me flush against his body.

*Breathtaking.*

Until I break it off, terrified by this desperate feeling swelling inside my chest.

*Suffocating.*

As what just happened slowly dawns on me.

I retract my hands from around his neck, placing them on his chest, an attempt to get some distance in between us.

Yet the harder I push, the firmer the fingertips of his hands on my lower back dig deeper into my skin, keeping me exactly in place.

Out of the blue, he gives me a statement, a promise, no doubt. "You'll never kiss another guy."

"What?"

"We're not playing around anymore. You want me, and I want you."

I vigorously shake my head.

"Go ahead and deny it. Say whatever you want. I don't care. I don't believe the words you say; they're all lies. Your body speaks the truth," he says, looking deep into my eyes.

*No. No. No.*

My body's betraying me. It's been too long. I never thought I would crave it. But that's all this is—me wanting physical attention.

"Mason is like a brother to me. He knows what I want; your body knows what it wants. Don't put him in between us ever again. I won't walk away from him next time."

*Another vow.*

"I'm not dancing around any longer. Done with the distance between us." He pauses. "I've tried to stay away. It doesn't work. I'm done backing down. We'll find a way."

I take in all his words, his last sentence, and more specifically, the word *we* awakens my defenses.

When I push harder against his chest, he gives me a little more breathing space, our bodies slightly apart, yet his arms remain around my waist, his hands unmovable.

"I'm a girl. I have needs. That's all this was," I try to explain.

His eyes flash dangerously while I see him biting back a few words before he answers, "Whatever lets you sleep at night, Lauren."

"We don't match. We hate each other. There will never be an *us* or a *we*," I continue with a higher voice, as if somebody were choking me.

"You're right. We're not the same. And I've fought our attraction as hard as you have." He pauses. "Maybe in different ways, but we've both tried to keep a distance, and we've both ended up doing stupid fucking things. You kissing Mason. And me wanting to strangle my own family for kissing you first." He sighs, his finger tilting my chin up. "I'll give you some time, but while I'm waiting, don't waste your energy in pushing me away. It won't work. Because I won't let you."

As soon as he lets go of my chin, I turn my head, staring off into the distance as he walks past me.

I'm still processing his words and the fact that I just had the most mind-blowing kiss ever. Considering I've kissed quite a few guys, that says *a lot.*

"Here." Coming to stand next to me, he holds out my helmet.

"I'm not getting back on *that thing*," I declare, looking up into his eyes, which are glazing with a new color, another side of him. "I'll walk." *To the nearest gas station and hitchhike from there.*

"I've been driving *that thing* for over four years. Trust me, nothing will happen. I promise," he assures me in the softest voice I've heard from him, the helmet still dangling in front of me.

Assessing him with wary eyes, I realize the most terrifying thing isn't getting on that bike, speeding through traffic.

It's him and whatever *this* is that scares the life out of me.

"Let's go," he says, losing his patience as he shoves the helmet into my arms.

Gazing around, I see no gas station or a possibility out of here, and even if there were, I can't overlook the wall of muscle on my right.

So, I grab the helmet, get on his bike, and curl my hands around the rail behind me.

"I just promised you, nothing would happen. You holding on to that isn't going to work," he says as he gets on. He really does his best not to sound pissed off, but it's not hard to figure out that he's not happy with what I'm doing. "Or do you want me to take off like before?"

I give him a death stare, which is rather pointless with my helmet on and his back to me. Yet I do value my life, so I shift a little closer while I'm still able to keep ahold of the rail behind me.

That is, until he revs the engine, the high-pitched sound piercing through the air, and I end up with my arms wrapped around him before he shoots off.

Five minutes later, I can absolutely confirm that he's incapable of driving slow. Although it isn't like before. With a lack of near collisions, my body is more relaxed while I let myself enjoy the view and the rush of adrenaline sizzling through my veins.

Taking the elevator back up to the apartment goes without talking. With me standing close to the wall and him close to the door, I get some breathing space, although he can't hide the scowl on his face, which reminds me of the promise he made.

*"I'll give you some time."*

*Time.*

It's what I need to build a new solid wall, high enough to block his advances and to trap the memory of that passionate kiss. Because forgetting seems almost impossible.

When the elevator doors open, he gets out first, noticing our small welcome committee, consisting of Matthew and Mason, who are awaiting us.

Mason walks up to us, glancing me up and down before he fixes his blue eyes on *him* as *he* moves in front of me.

"Are you out of your mind?" Mason snaps.

*This isn't going to end well.*

"What's the problem?" *he* asks, eerily calm while his body tenses up.

Matthew nears us, perfectly aware of the upcoming thunderstorm.

"*You're* my problem! Driving off with her on the back of your bike in the middle of the night without any backup! What about her safety, the risks you're taking?" he hisses, breathing heavily. "Deal with your issues on your own instead of dragging her along, risking her life in the process!"

"I would never risk her life, and you know it!" *he* fires back, taking a step closer to Mason. "But that's not really what's bothering you, is it?"

"Liam," Matthew warns, standing close to the side, ready to jump in.

"What? You think I want to kiss her again?" Mason challenges when *he* takes the final step, their faces now merely inches from each other.

*Oh boy. That's my cue.*

Coming to stand right next to *him*—since there's no place in between them—I yelp, "Stop this bullshit."

Their standoff remains while their eyes are focused on each other.

Unable to solve what I've caused, I say to no one in particular, "I'm going to bed."

I won't stick around to watch them kill each other.

Ridiculous.

Meaningless.

Their fight for someone who isn't even on the market in the first place.

# CHAPTER 25
## VANCE

It's the middle of the night when my cell phone starts ringing.

"What's wrong?" I snap, accepting the call.

"Sorry to disturb you at this hour—"

"I don't care." Sleep isn't important; her safety is. "Is she—"

"She's fine," he assures me, soothing my anxious mind just a bit.

But I'm getting ticked off with the way he's prolonging this conversation. "Tell me."

"He's made his move."

Those words have more power than a slap in the face, and a sudden need to strangle William Drew Ressler with my bare hands overwhelms me.

"When?"

"There was a party—"

"A party?" I hiss, interrupting him for the second time.

"It was perfectly safe." He pauses. "Long story short, he kissed her, and now, he's made it very clear." Another pause. "He's not holding back anymore."

It's enough information for me to make my decision. "I'm done with SPISe."

"They're doing a great job. But I don't think she's—"

A decision I didn't expect he would question. "So, you're telling me, you can screw a girl and protect her at the same time?"

No answer.

*Exactly.*

"Give me a time and a place, and I'll be there."

"Will do."

# Chapter 26
## LAUREN

My hair is the first thing I notice when I open my eyes. As I lie on my stomach, it's draped all over my face.

I'm not a peaceful sleeper; I'm more of a tornado in bed. One who tends to snooze a lot. So, I close my eyes and wriggle my body a little more under the blankets until I notice I'm stuck. Something's blocking me from moving freely.

"Lie still, will you?"

My eyes pop open, my body tensing, while I wait and pray it was a hallucination, like the ones you have when you're drifting in between dream and reality, unable to figure out which is which.

To confirm I'm not dreaming, I push myself upward, and I notice I can't even bring myself to do so. Something's not only blocking my moves; it's holding me down.

My breath hitches as a survival instinct starts kicking in. Pushing harder, I finally succeed in getting myself in a position where I'm upright on my knees while I stare at the cause of my problem.

*He's* propped on one elbow, which accentuates his bare chest and his chiseled abs.

I'm suddenly wide-awake.

Seeing *him*.

In my bed.

Half-naked.

My mind fries as I stare, dumbfounded.

"Something wrong?" He smirks with sleepy eyes, demanding my attention back on his face.

*Get a grip, Lauren.*

And I do, literally, as I grasp my pillow and throw it in his face, afraid to touch him even if it is to strangle him.

"What the hell are you doing here?" I yell. "What's wrong with *your* bed?" I point at the empty bed a few feet away, the one Mason has been using for the past few weeks, the one *he's* used before.

Stuffing the *handed* pillow underneath his head, he lies back down, making himself all too comfortable.

"I told you, I'm done keeping my distance. Now, go back to sleep," he says casually while he folds his hands beneath his head.

"Out!" And, when he doesn't react, I yell, "Now!"

He doesn't budge.

Not. A. Single. Muscle.

I shove aside the sheets pooled around my waist and jump out of bed.

*There's absolutely no way I can go back to sleep.*

I snatch a pair of jeans and a shirt out of the closet and stomp out of the bedroom, cursing myself that I didn't stick around last night when Mason was facing off with *him.*

I could've supported Mason in chasing him away.

And yet, I didn't.

# Chapter 27
## LAUREN

The walls used to be my cage, something I wanted to escape from. Now, it's become a person. Someone who's getting too close, demanding something I can't give *him* or any other guy.

And, while I try to convince him that he's barking up the wrong tree, it doesn't stop him from shadowing my every move during the day or sleeping in my room every night. Although he's back to sleeping in his own bed.

Enduring his behavior and trying to keep my grief nicely stashed away has given me quite an edge. One that hasn't gone unnoticed by anyone, including Dr. Jemerson—the therapist I've been seeing since I arrived in New York.

Before, I had no clue how an overpaid man could help. But, now that he's seeing things my way, a person who acknowledges and supports my need to exercise *outside*, I've changed my mind about him and his profession.

"So, are you up for it?" Sarah asks, fully dressed in her sports attire, ready for what's probably her first official run outside. She's willing to sacrifice her dignity for the sake of me.

"Absolutely." *It's been too long.* "You?"

"I've never done this." She fiddles with her hair. "I'll probably slow you down."

"Trust me, jogging with you will be ten thousand times more fun than running with them." I point at the happy bunch, containing Matthew, Mason, and *him*, who are huddled in the kitchen area, discussing what seems to be serious business. "I don't care how fast we're going. As long as you can produce more than a grim face, it'll be perfect." I wink.

I'm normally a person who feeds on speed, but when I have to run with people who kill my zone every five seconds, then I'll gladly run with Sarah instead.

"Are you girls ready?" Mason asks, trying to sound laid-back.

I can tell he's nervous, as his freshly washed hair is already out of order.

"Let's just go." I really don't know what all this fuss is about.

Just as I thought it couldn't get any worse, another black-hooded runner walks into our penthouse.

"Really?" I exclaim, shaking my head while I seriously start to reconsider this offer.

"The more, the merrier. Right?" Jaden says with a smile on his face.

*Yeah.*

I've recently deleted that phrase out of my personal dictionary.

*There's really no such thing.*

Taking a different car—a black Ford SUV that can fit all six of us with room to spare—to go out for a run is freaking ridiculous. But, of course, it's not up for discussion. Of all the things I've learned, it's best not to fight four brooding, black-hooded men when they're doing me a favor.

With Sarah sitting next to me, I'm able to keep my completely reasonable comments to myself. Still, twenty minutes later, my anxiousness takes over.

"Where are we going?" I ask Matthew, who's riding shotgun.

I refuse to ask *him*. I know he won't give me an answer.

"We're almost there."

*Splendid.* "There being ..."

"A park outside the city."

That's when I'm done with keeping my opinion to myself. "Why would we drive half an hour when we have a park a block away?"

"Don't want to be predictable," Matthew clips while *he* keeps his eyes on the street, full work mode on.

I take a deep breath while I reminisce about the time when running used to be so simple.

"Just follow us, and all will be well," Matthew explains with a strained voice.

And, just like swimming, they have no clue what exercising is all about.


"They forgot to send us the memo to dress in black," I joke when I get out of the car, the four of them surrounding us, as Sarah's pink sweater and my red hoodie clearly stand out.

"I hate black," Sarah announces.

I'm not surprised. She's too bright on the inside to wear a dark, gloomy color. I, on the other hand, love black, but I'm really glad I didn't pick it for today.

"Matthew and I are going to run in front of you guys. Jaden and Mason will be behind you. Just stay in between us," *he* coordinates.

*Oh. Boy.*

I'm not sure if I'll ever run again after this. Still, for Sarah's sake, I do as we were told, running in between the four of them, which feels absolutely ridiculous. I'm sure the president's run is more satisfying than mine.

When I look on the bright side—which is in fact Sarah on my left side—she manages to temper my frustrations and the urge to run the hell away.

"Are you hanging in there?" I ask, coaching my saving grace.

"Yes," she huffs, giving me a forced smile while her head is glowing red and her breath is out of control after only six minutes of running.

She's dying—or at least, that's how she most likely feels.

"Let's take a break," I suggest, taking her arm while I slow down to a walking pace.

As if *he* and Matthew have eyes on their backs, they start to walk, followed by a wary look from Matthew toward Sarah.

*Seriously, the guy needs to back down.*

I shake my head, showing him the palm of my hand so that he doesn't move toward us. He continues his conversation with *him*, leaving it be. At least, for now.

"Breathe in through your nose and out through your mouth," I instruct her.

"God, I'm slowing you down. You're not even sweating yet," she pants.

"Hey, I didn't start out this way. I was once like you. If you really want this, I'm sure you'll end up just like me. It's all about practice and endurance."

"Right. Maybe I should start with going to our fitness room instead. That way, I won't keep you from running."

"What? A fitness room? No one's ever told me about that." *Probably on purpose.*

"Yes, we have one for our employees. It's on the first floor. I've seen it but never used it. Matthew doesn't approve since almost every employee in the building is a man."

*No surprise there.*

"He shouldn't stop you from doing something you like."

"He cares about me," she says with pride.

"I'm absolutely certain he means well, but he loves you too much sometimes. Love shouldn't involve restricting each other at any time—" I stop giving her a lecture once I notice the large frown on her face, and a pang of guilt hits me in the chest.

*Who am I to shove my values down her throat?*

"You know what? Forget what I said. I think you two are a great couple. I don't want you to do things because I say so. If you want to do something you like and Matthew doesn't really like it, you can always ask me for help but only if *you* want it," I point out.

Smiling at me, she agrees, "Okay, I can do that. Maybe starting off on the treadmill is a good idea."

"Then, that's what we'll do. So, what do you say? Are we going to run again, or are we going to chill on this bench over here?" I ask, coming to a standstill.

"Let's just take a seat for a moment. I don't know if I can do this again," she admits.

I'm glad she's being honest with me.

"You should probably stretch a little. Otherwise, you'll end up waking in the morning with a sudden need to kill me." I smirk.

I show her some great stretching exercises for her legs and arms while our national guard takes post at either side of us.

Mason and Jaden are stretching alongside a tree. *He* and Matthew are clearly in a heated conversation, according to *his* grim face and Matthew's distinct arm gestures. The moment I shift my gaze back to Sarah sitting on the ground, I notice some movement in the background.

As Matthew promised, this park has in fact been deserted—until now, as I notice a stranger approaching us. Even though he's not nearly that close, he's on the same path we just took. It's only a matter of time before he passes us.

I'm the last person to freak out, but I must admit, he does look rather suspicious, wearing dark clothing and a cap that covers up his face.

Me worrying a little equals four guys on high alert.

Matthew and *he* are already approaching us, being the furthest away from the running stranger. Jaden and Mason decide to stretch in the middle of the path, trying to force the guy to run over the grass, further away from Sarah and me.

"Stay behind me," *he* instructs, planting his body right in front of me.

Matthew makes his way over to Sarah, hugging her to his left side.

For once, I'm grateful he's overprotective.

Everyone's on edge, including me, but I'm the only one who has the need to cut the tension with a snide remark. "Is there actually a guy running in this public park? What the hell is he thinking?"

No response, all eyes set on the incoming jogger, who passes Mason and Jaden before he runs right past us.

"See, just a man going for—"

I stop mid-sentence as a slow-motion movie starts playing out, starting with this man abruptly turning around before he heads straight toward us.

Toward me.

I wanted to go out for a run. I begged for it, and now, I've endangered everyone by coming here.

Nobody can get hurt.

Not because of me.

Not again.

So, I do the only thing that makes perfect sense right now. I slip beneath *his* outstretched arm, giving the man exactly what he wants.

Me.

# Chapter 28
## LIAM

I'm normally not the guy to say *I told you so*.

Not the person to have this urge to shove it in someone else's face when I'm right.

And yet, today is again a day of another first.

Still, my need to do just that has taken a backseat, as I'm too busy keeping myself from strangling her for being her. So. Fucking. Stupid.

Yet my emotions are an obstacle.

Insignicant. Dangerous.

Knowing who's at risk here, I contain them, focusing on what I do best—protect her stubborn ass. I counter her brainless move by clasping my left hand around her arm while my right hand reaches out for the gun tucked in the back of my pants, pointing it at the foolish man who thinks he can take her away from me. "Let her go."

Jaden and Mason have taken position on either side of the stranger. He's completely surrounded, at least three guns set on him while he still has his hand on her arm, similar to my hold.

"Release her," Mason commands as he shoves his gun deeper into the side of the stranger.

And he lets go.

Yet another demonstration of the persuasiveness of a gun, the reason we carry. And, even if it's fucking uncomfortable while running, I'd do it again in a heartbeat if it gets her safely in my arms.

Pulling her to my chest, my left arm clasped around her waist, I step back while my gun remains trained on him.

With his hands in the air, he finally decides to reveal his face, hidden by a baseball cap.

The man shocks all of us, including Lauren, who wobbles on her feet.

"Vance," Matthew clips as he comes to stand next to me.

I haven't restrained as much emotion in my lifetime as I've done this past year. But I'd rather support Lauren than attack him for being a fucked up parent, for making all the wrong decisions, for endangering *her.*

While Mason and Jaden keep him under shot, I see Max and Bryan arriving—our backup car for today—and I tuck away my gun, so I can use both arms to hold Lauren, keeping her from staggering to the ground.

She lets me, if only for a few seconds, before I feel her gaining strength, before her chest swells as she fights my restraint, her hands going for the man she barely knows, her father who ruined her life.

"You bastard! You killed her!"

I would love to grant her this, let her go so that she can get rid of her anger. It would be more effective than all her therapy sessions. But I have no clue what he's capable of, and it's a risk I'm not willing to take.

So, I hug her close to my chest as I take another step back while I whisper her name close to her ear.

Unlike me, her feelings aren't easily contained; they're out on full display.

"You took away my sister!"

"Lauren," he commences, "I'm sorry."

As he takes a step closer, Jaden and Mason hold him back.

"Shut up!"

"Lauren, let me explain," he pleads.

Her breathing erratic, she goes on, "I don't want to hear it! You're dead to me!"

It's enough for him to realize she's beyond comprehension. Shifting his attention to me, boring his eyes into mine, he demands an even more foolish suggestion, "I want to talk to her alone."

"Not gonna happen," I hiss, taking another step back with Lauren's body still plastered to mine.

"Come on, let's take a walk," Jaden suggests, his hand pushing Vance back.

"She's my daughter! You have no right to keep her from me!" he shouts, fighting both Mason's and Jaden's hold.

"Calm down, Vance," Matthew commands, grabbing ahold of his shoulder. "I thought we agreed that we would take care of Lauren while you handled the threat. Let us. You're not thinking straight, risking her life in the process."

"I am thinking straight, and I see her in the hands of a kid who's far from able to keep her safe."

"He got admitted to the Army but declined because he wanted to do this. He took all the necessary courses. He's more than capable of keeping her safe. I trust him completely," he states. "Besides, this isn't a one-man job, as you can see."

With Matthew busy calming Vance, I put more distance in between us while Lauren's hazel eyes connect with mine.

"Let me go."

Even though it's with a soft, pleading voice, I can't give in.

"I'm fine," she insists.

Yet again, her words are meaningless. I can still feel her tense body against mine. She's not fine at all. Add the fact that we've been standing still for too long without knowing how Vance found us here, it's enough for me to get a move on things.

"Let's get you back to the car. Can you walk?"

Instead of giving me an answer, she glares at her father, still close enough for him to hear her say, "You didn't just kill my sister; you murdered the both of us. I died the day I lost the only family I had left." Her voice is eerily calm before she turns around in my arms, saying, "Let's go."

I guide her away, her body close to my side, my arm around her middle, when Mason appears on her other side.

"The car is over there." Bryan, coming to walk beside me, points out the black Range Rover parked along the curb at the edge of the park.

Glancing backward, I see Matthew and Jaden talking to Vance while Max is guiding Sarah back to the other car. They've got the situation under control.

*Good.*

Setting eyes back on the car, I pick up the pace. Every step we take makes Lauren breathe harder, gasping for another breath, as if we were running a marathon when we're only strolling.

She's done this before—hyperventilating while she's lost in her mind. Whatever is going on in that head of hers, it surely isn't good, and if she doesn't snap out of it, I'll be driving her to the fucking hospital, which is the last place I want her to be right now.

Halting in the middle of the lawn, I pull her back to my front—one hand on her chest, the other on her stomach. "I've got you, Lauren. Just breathe in slowly," I whisper, my chin on her shoulder. "And breathe out," I continue as my hands slowly push inward.

Of course, she fights it. At first. But I refuse to give in. I keep doing the same thing over and over again until her breathing starts to follow the rhythm I'm indicating. Until she gives in, letting me take care of her. With her wall down and my urge to get out of here ASAP, I don't hesitate to pick her up before I cradle her body close to mine. A vulnerable position, one she normally wouldn't allow. Except for now.

With her eyes closed, we reach the car in record time. Bryan takes position behind the wheel, and Mason opens the back door before he reclines the seat, so I'm able to place her in it, buckling her in before I slam the door.

"I'm going to kill that bastard," I hiss, taking a step in the direction where we came from, ready to commit murder. For Lauren. And for Kate.

"Don't!" Mason's hand around my arm stops me from moving forward while his left hand stops Bryan from getting out of the car. "She needs you right now."

Even though Mason and Bryan would never be able to stop me physically, not when I'm determined like I am right now.

It's his words that urge me to stay. It's his message that keeps me here, with her.

He used to be the one to look out for her. But, now, I've taken on that role.

And I won't fail her. Ever. Again.

# CHAPTER 29
## LAUREN

*He* carried me to the car, and I let him.

I was in his arms when we took the elevator, and I never complained.

He helped me into my nightwear and crawled into bed with me, and I didn't say a word.

Because I can't.

As much as I don't want anybody's help, as much as I hate to open up to others, I can't seem to push him away.

I had it all under control.

Keeping *him* at a certain distance.

My sister pushed to the far corner of my mind.

It worked—until today when Vance stood in front of me and ruined it all. When flashes of my sister's lifeless body flooded my mind, destroying me all over again.

Gazing at the deep blue curtains covering the floor-to-ceiling windows—the ones that Liam closed because it's still light out—I will myself to sleep by reliving every beautiful memory I can remember with my sister.

All those times we both slept in her tiny bed even though one of us was doomed to fall out during the night. The countless weekends spent together, hanging around the beach to avoid my mother's crazy boyfriends. The numerous times of climbing out our window and down our old oak tree in the front yard to sneak out.

The more I'm flooded with precious memories, the more my eyes risk spilling those dreadful tears.

Still, I manage to keep them at bay for now, too busy breathing away my nauseousness. Yet there's no relief, and I do the one thing I seem to do so well lately.

I start to panic.

Tearing my mind away from *her*, I try to conjure happy thoughts, ones that don't involve my sister. But it's too late. I'm drowning, and as badly as I want to remain quiet, I can't do it while I'm freaking out.

"Fuck, Lauren," Liam curses.

Even though he initially kept his distance, lying in my bed without him touching me, an arm snakes underneath my body, another arm curling around my waist. He pulls me into a sitting position, doing the exact same thing he did this afternoon as he places a hand on my chest and one on my stomach.

"I'm here."

The moment those words leave his mouth, my very unstable wall crumbles to the ground, my breath completely out of control as I bawl my eyes out.

"I've got you," he repeats, doing the same movement with his hands over and over again.

Once my breathing takes on a steady rhythm, we sink deeper underneath the sheets, shifting to our sides, my body pressed against his.

And I realize ... I'm lying in Liam's arms.

The guy who I vowed to never say or even think his name.

The only reason I'm able to breathe normally.

# CHAPTER 30
## LAUREN

I haven't had a decent night of sleep since I've been here. Not one without the help of my sleeping pills.

Yet, tonight, I've slept for nine hours straight without a single nightmare.

As much as I want to deny the real reason, I feel the palm of *his* hand beneath my shirt, pressing against my skin, and the warmth of his body along my back.

It feels right. But it scares me more.

That's why I'm trying to slip out of his hold, craving a nice long shower, a good distance away from him to figure all of this out.

"Lauren?"

I've just managed to get my body out from beneath his arm when he grabs ahold of my hand.

"What are you doing?"

With him holding my hand, I still try to get up, but he just pulls me back onto the bed.

"It's five thirty in the morning. Just lie down with me for a bit longer."

Shaking my head, I tell him, "I'm going to go shower." I give it another try, but I land back on the bed with a bounce.

"Talk to me," he pleads.

Shaking my head, I feel his hand loosening. And I use that very moment to pull out of his grasp before I head for the closest door, which is toward the hallway and not to the bathroom. Pulling it open, I'm about to slip out when a hand slams against the door, closing it in front of my face.

"I know what you're trying to do," he states, the slightest bit of anger lingering in the background.

Whether it's the lack of speech or me keeping my back to him, I don't know, but he connects the dots way too fast.

Turning around, I face his shirt instead of his eyes, using the same excuse. "I want to go take a shower."

"*The shower* is that way," he states, indicating the door behind him and not the one I was about to use. He continues, "You want to run."

He knows.

Yet I can't stop myself from ducking beneath his arm, which is still glued to the door, and I head toward the bathroom.

Wishing he'd stop figuring me out.

Stop crawling beneath my skin.

"Let's talk about *this*," he urges, his voice an olive branch, as he follows right behind, doing the exact same thing with the bathroom door when I try to open it.

While he's softening his voice, mine is gaining in strength. "I need to shower," I demand, ducking under his arms once again, heading for the window, as if it were a possible exit when it grants me only some distance away from him.

"I saw something yesterday." His voice is low and fierce, his words filled with so much promise that a buzz flitters over my skin. One I try to ignore while I focus on my mission.

I take off my right sock, flinging it away.

Suspiciously gazing at me, he continues, "I saw a glimpse of the real Lauren. The one you've been hiding so well."

Another sock flies across the room.

"I knew she was in there. I never doubted that. But I finally got to see it with my own fucking eyes."

My stomach contracts while I try to focus on my fingers clutching the rim of my pajama shorts.

"You mind?" I huff, wanting his butt out the door while I'm stripping down my shorts.

Instead, his dark eyes narrow to thin slits.

"I've seen a piece," he says.

I kick my shorts away.

His brooding, dark eyes shimmer while he follows my every move, waiting for my eyes to connect with his before he finishes it off, "Now, I want it all."

There's that buzz again, sizzling through my veins, spreading in a matter of seconds, as my body is aching for another mind-blowing kiss, another touch, the warmth of his skin pressing against mine.

*How many times do I have to fight myself because of this guy?*

Rendered speechless, I continue my onslaught, taking off my shirt before I end up in a black sports bra and black panties. Unashamed, I stare him down. It's not like he hasn't seen me like this; he undressed me yesterday.

"What are you doing?" he asks, slowly approaching me.

Since the door is on the other side of the room, I've got nowhere to go. I can only try to suppress my deer-in-the-headlights reaction as he covers a few more feet.

"Don't ask me for something you don't want," he threatens.

*Did I just do that? Has my body taken over control?*

As I'm frozen on the spot, he covers the distance until he's only inches away.

I should push him back, but my hands won't cooperate. His presence does something to my body, and it's getting worse when his stare becomes one with an undeniable, raw intensity. Yet, somehow, he's the one holding back as he tucks a strand of hair behind my ear before his fingertips slide downward, tracing my neck and collarbone. A touch so gentle, it blinds my fury, chasing away the ghosts that haunt me.

Closing my eyes, I let myself enjoy every second of it while he goes on. Brushing my hair from my shoulder, he starts kissing the same trail he just did with his finger while his arms encircle my lower body, tucking it closer to the safety of his.

Letting him support me, I lean my head slightly back.

"God, Lauren. What you do to me."

My eyes pop open, my body tensing at the sound of my name on his lips.

Something that's foreign to my ears.

I never give my name to a guy I'm intimate with.

It's way too personal.

"I need to pee."

"Lauren," he threatens.

"I really have to go," I beg now.

He remains in the same position for a second longer.

Hesitating.

Before his arms fall away.

When I have free passage to leave, I dart to the bathroom and lock myself in. Pressing my body against the door, I slowly slide down until my body hits the ground.

I remind myself, even though it's cold and lonely on planet Lauren, at least it's safe.

# Chapter 31
## LAUREN

Showers aren't the solution.

Neither is trying to ignore *him*, which is nearly impossible anyway.

The only solution that might help seems to be the only thing he absolutely doesn't want.

I remember the fantastic conversation we had about it yesterday morning.

*"I want to go out for a run," I stated as I was sitting on the marble kitchen island, my feet pushed back against the counter, while he was sitting on a barstool five feet away.*

*Without a glance my way, a, "No," was the only thing I got as he kept his head down, eyes glued to his tablet while he took a bite off his sandwich.*

*Ever since I'd increased my defenses—or more like avoided him as much as possible—he'd been like this, always in my vicinity, a permanent scowl plastered on his face.*

*My hands holding the rim of the marble counter, I squeezed it a little harder as I tried to keep my calm. "Excuse me?"*

*"No more running outside. Do I need to remind you of what happened last time?" he scoffed, still not facing me.*

*No, he didn't have to remind me; it was embedded into my brain.*

*"Fine, it's settled then. I'll use the gym on the first floor," I declared, jumping off the counter.*

*"Out of the question," he barked, his dark eyes boring into mine.*

*"It's in the building. Members only."* Thank you, Sarah, for telling me. *"They're all in the security business. I couldn't be safer."*

*"I don't fucking care. I don't know them, so I don't trust them," he stated with a this-is-basic-knowledge look.*

*"Either I go for a run in the park or I run in the gym."* Even though I'd rather not swim, I could still use it to push him in the right direction. *"I can't drown while I'm running."*

*That was when he graced me with that death stare of his.*

*"By the way, Dr. Jemerson said that running is an excellent way to handle my anxiety."*

*Instead of a crude response, he shoved his plate to the side, got up, and stomped toward the elevator.*

*Perfect. So, we had an understanding.*


"You girls ready?" Mason asks, walking into the room, his baseball cap twisted backward, his dark gray pants hanging from his waist, a white shirt on top.

"Absolutely." I smile when Sarah just nods, twiddling with her braid.

Mason squeezes her shoulder. "Is Matthew okay with this?"

"I just called to let him know. He doesn't mind as long as you tag along."

He nods before his piercing blue eyes focus on me. "You sure *Liam* knows about this?" He emphasizes *his* name.

"Yes." *He's been informed; he just doesn't approve. But I want—no, I need a chance to prove nothing will happen.*

The frown on Mason's forehead increases as he takes his phone out of his pocket. "He's still not picking up his phone."

*I might've accidentally put his phone on Airplane Mode this morning when I switched off his alarm.*

"Half an hour, tops. Besides, it's in the building, and you're coming along. What could go wrong?" I throw back.

He takes off his cap, and his hand goes through his hair before he puts it back on, sending another desperate look to the outside world before he grabs my hand and pulls me along. "If Liam kills me, I'm haunting you night *and* day!"

*Oh boy.*

The gym is on the first floor. Sliding a key card through an electronic slot, Mason pushes open the door to reveal an entire floor filled with tons of fitness gear. They could easily train an army in here.

"So, what are we going to do first?" Mason asks.

*We?*

Turning my head toward him, I state, "We"—I indicate Sarah and myself—"want to work out alone." *No way will he follow us everywhere we go.*

Mason looks us up and down, his gaze lingering just a bit longer on me, before he sets his eyes back on the fitness room. "You don't leave this room or go to the toilet without me knowing."

"Done," I agree.

Before he has a chance to make other demands, I snatch two bottles of water from a nearby table, giving one to Sarah before I pull her along in the direction of the treadmills.

Placing the bottle of water on the ground next to my treadmill, I ask, "You know how to set it?" I step onto the running belt.

"Yes, no problem. Matthew showed me," she says, increasing the speed of her treadmill.

I pick up speed, too, but I make sure I'm still able to talk while running.

"So, how did you persuade Liam to let you do this?" Sarah asks, already a little out of breath.

Keeping information from Mason is one thing, but when I consider lying to Sarah, my tongue refuses to cooperate. "I didn't."

"What?" she shrieks.

"Shh," I hush, refraining myself from putting my finger to my lips as I search for Mason, who's lifting weights halfway across the room. Only with Superman hearing could he have heard.

"Liam's going to be furious," she whispers, worrying for the both of us.

"When is *he* not?" I scoff. "Besides, he can't keep me locked up; it's not even necessary. I'll prove it. Nothing will happen," I explain.

A silence settles between us.

Only the rhythm of our feet descending on the running belts is audible.

"He loves you," she says out of the blue.

I almost miss a step when her words sift through my mind, trying to fit in somewhere when I can't even begin to comprehend them in the first place.

"The way he's hovering, the need he has to be everywhere you are, you're more to *him*."

I don't know how to respond to that. I just let the information seep in.

"Can I ask you something?"

I guess my silence has made her insecure.

"Sure."

*It can't get much worse.*

"Have you ever been in love with someone?"

Easy question to answer. "Nope, and I never plan to."

"It must have been hard, losing your mom," she says right before she looks up at me with a worried expression, as if she hadn't meant to say it out loud.

"We managed." I shrug while, on the inside, a knot is forming, enough for me to pick up speed. *If only I could physically run away from my past.*

"I haven't seen you girls around," a male voice next to me speaks up.

So lost down memory lane, I didn't notice him taking the treadmill next to me.

"Well, actually, I haven't seen many girls around here," he confesses.

"Things are about to change." I wink at Sarah, who's getting a bit uncomfortable.

"Glad to hear it."

I take another look at him while he starts to run, a little relieved that he didn't just come for smooth talk. But then, from the corner of my eye, I see someone approaching.

Lifting up my hand in a subtle way, I look at Mason, his playful side completely gone, as he's seconds away from handling this guy, who isn't even a threat. Nothing I can't manage.

I give him another shake of my head, which stops him in his tracks.

It's enough of a warning for him to get on a treadmill the farthest away from us, his scolding blue eyes set on us.

"What department do you two work for?"

"HR," I explain, giving Sarah a look. She shakes her head in the smallest, subtlest way. "You?"

"Nice. I'm a field operative. Mostly out there unless I'm working out."

He starts explaining how he got the job in the first place when a male voice booms behind me. "What the hell are you doing?"

*I swear, the guy has an app for my whereabouts.*

"What does it look like I'm doing?" I fume as I give a sideways glance, noticing *his* white-knuckled hand is curled around my handrail, every muscle in his arm accentuated.

"Get off," he commands.

I shake my head, my ponytail swaying over my shoulders as I pick up the pace. That is, until the running belt stops abruptly, the safety plug no longer in its rightful place.

"Get. Off."

I notice the muscles in his arm flexing.

He's holding himself back. *Barely.*

"Do you know him?" The stranger interferes, his eyes zeroing in on me.

A possible lifeline, but it's really not. I want to come back here, and I want this stranger to be able to walk and talk like a normal person. That's the only reason I step off the running belt and pick up my water bottle.

Before I'm able to unscrew the cap, the bottle is snatched out of my hands.

"And what the hell are you wearing?" *he* spits out, looking at one spot in particular—my cleavage.

It's not on display, although my loose shirt might have given the stranger and *him* a nice view as I picked up my bottle just now.

Without a word, *he* throws the water bottle in Mason's direction before he pulls his black hoodie over his head in one swift move and shoves it into my arms.

His message is crystal clear.

I've reached my boiling point, balancing on the edge, when I remind myself what's at stake here. I can't lose my cool. I can't ruin this even more. That's why I pull his freaking hoodie over my head, my facial expression promising hell. *Later.*

"What the fuck, man? Stop bullying her like that," the stranger says as he steps off his treadmill, entering the war zone. "Leave her alone," he continues.

*He's* been ignoring him, targeting me.

Until now when he turns his body around.

*Oh boy.*

"Are you her boyfriend or something?" the guy scoffs.

I hesitate, trying to think of something, when *he* opens his mouth.

"I'm the one who's sleeping in her bed every night," he declares.

Suddenly, the word *boyfriend* sounds a hundred times better. I'm reminded of my weakness, my inability to push him away, especially at night when I have no energy left, exhausted from the many nightmares and the panic attacks that come with it.

"Well then, you're doing a terrible job," the smart—or rather, very stupid—man remarks.

If it wasn't for Mason's impeccable timing, getting in between *him* and the guy, he would have lost his teeth already.

"Let's go," Mason suggests as he pushes *him* slightly back.

Another five seconds tick by before *he* shifts his eyes to Mason, jabbing a finger into his chest. "This is on you," he states firmly.

I grind my teeth while I swallow down the guilt of getting them into a fight again. I know this is all on me. Yet there's nothing I can do, as I've learned so much from the past.

I head toward the exit where Matthew is talking to Sarah.

I plan to walk past them, but Matthew grabs ahold of my arm, giving me a grim look.

"We go up together."

Sharing a look with Sarah, I see guilt written all over her face even though she's done nothing wrong. Sending her a reassuring smile, I lean my back against the wall.

A few minutes later, we all pile into the elevator.

Absolute silence.

As if we're caught in the eye of the storm.

Until we reach our floor.

Mason is the first to walk out, followed by *him*, and last but not least, me. Surprisingly, Matthew and Sarah remain in the elevator.

"What the hell were you thinking, taking her there?" *he* demands as Mason walks toward the kitchen.

"She deserves to run, Liam," he answers, turning around, facing *him*.

"No, she deserves to live another day," *he* barks as he leans closer to Mason's face.

*Is he serious? We are inside a secure building.*

Mason remains calm as he says, "You're overreacting."

*Thank you, Mason.*

"I don't fucking care if I'm overreacting. I'm here to keep her alive."

"I was there to make sure of that."

"Then, where the hell were you when that guy was all over her?" *he* shoots back.

*All over me? The guy didn't even touch me!*

"She doesn't leave the apartment without me ever again," *he* barks the command as if he were in charge here.

*Yeah, that's my cue.*

"Stop being an overbearing asshole. Nothing happened," I scream as I get in between them again.

But, just like last time, I might as well be air.

"Whatever." I throw my hands in the air, about to leave, but I've got one more thing to say. "As for the 'one who's sleeping in her bed every night,' don't even try it if you want to keep your manhood intact," I warn before I stomp down the hall toward my room, remembering Mason's promise.

*"If Liam kills me, I'm haunting you night and day!"*

Yep, I'm doomed to be haunted by Mason, the—hopefully—friendly ghost.

# CHAPTER 32
## LIAM

Lauren is in her room, her favorite space to run to, the only place she has that gives some semblance of privacy.

As much as she thinks I don't understand her need to run, I do. But the urge to keep her safe from Frank Calvetti, from her own father, is an absolute priority. Because, right now, we're grasping at straws on what they're up to. We still have no clue how Vance knew where to find us. Is he tracking us in some way? Or worse, do we have a mole working among us?

The thought alone has me worrying day and night.

Reason enough to be extra cautious. Or as Mason likes to call it, overreacting. The less people who know about her being here, the better. Including the ones working in this building.

So, I'll happily deal with Lauren's feisty behavior.

I won't hesitate to risk my manhood.

All of it is a minor annoyance in comparison to the risk of losing her.

I can't bear the thought of her suffering through an anxiety attack alone, which she's had almost every night since our run in the park.

As expected, this night isn't any different. Only an hour later after I've crawled into her bed, her frail body starts twisting and turning as she's gasping for air.

"Relax," I whisper once she's sitting upright in bed. My hand caressing her sweat-covered-back, I give her a chance to snap out of it before I intervene.

She hasn't refused my help before, but today, her stubbornness shines through as she shies away from my touch before she slides out of bed.

Swallowing down my anger, I try to get her back by pleading, "Lauren, come back to bed."

That only makes it worse, and she retreats further away from it, from me, all the while urging her lungs to do their job.

Rising to my full height, I move toward her. She can't have her much-needed distance, not while she's suffocating.

"Stop being stubborn," I threaten, the edge in my voice unmistakable, as I'm unable to hide how pissed off I am at seeing her do this. "Let me help you."

Still, she retreats further until her back is up against the window. She holds up both hands, gasping. "I can do this."

She's never been able to get through this herself. And I've given her too much time and space already.

When I take a stand right in front of her, she raises the palms of her hands before they press against my chest. The touch of her hands calms me, encourages me to solve this with words one more time. "I never said you couldn't. But you don't have to do this alone."

Light from the hallway spills into the room, enough for me to see her press her lips together as she closes her eyes, shutting me out.

"You'd rather suffocate than let me help you?" I spit out.

She doesn't say a word. She doesn't need to; I already know the answer.

I'm seconds away from stepping in when her breathing starts to stabilize.

She opens her eyes. "I don't need you."

I wonder if she believes her own lies.

"Keep telling yourself that, but don't bother giving me that shit," I fume, my gaze shifting from her face and down to her hands. They're no longer pushing against my chest; instead, they're clutching my shirt, as if she were holding on for dear life.

She follows my gaze, looking down, and her eyes go wide. A mix of emotions swirling over her face, she retracts her hands, and her body turns rigid.

It's only a matter of seconds before she starts pushing me away again. Or worse, trying to slip away, as if nothing happened.

With her having a hard time lately, I've held my tongue too many times, but now, I'm going to have a word with her.

Or lots of them.

Slamming my hands against the window, I make sure she has nowhere to go. "We've got to talk."

"I have nothing to say."

"Perfect. You'll be a good listener then."

She scoffs.

"Ignoring me is one thing. Using Mason to get out of the apartment is another. But pushing me away when your health is on the line is a whole other issue. It'd better not happen again."

She shakes her head.

"As for the fitness room, you go running with me, or you don't go running at all."

"You're not the boss of me—"

"I thought you had nothing to say," I cut her off.

"You are—"

That smart mouth of hers.

I can't take it any longer.

I slam my mouth against hers.

She hesitates the first two seconds before she gives in, and I press her harder against the cold window, deepening our kiss.

Until I pull back, just a few inches.

Until I see her closed eyes, her lips parted, slightly panting.

As hard as it is to stop right here, I can't push it further.

I won't, not until she's fully into this.

"Let's go to bed."

Opening her eyes, she can barely keep her lips tight, her body gleaming from the aftermath.

Unlike her, I don't make any effort to stop the smile tugging at my lips.

"You're an ass," she snaps, pushing me back.

I retract my arms, grinning at her, unaffected by her words.

They're hollow.

Meaningless.

"So I've been told."

"Clearly not enough," she retorts as she stomps to the bed, making me want to kiss her mouth all over again.

Yet I let it go.

For now.

She matches my stubbornness, but the real question is, *Who will persevere?*

And, well, the fact is, I'm nowhere near tired.

# CHAPTER 33
## LAUREN

Of all days, I should've known Greg would pick today to come and visit me. A day I've been dreading for weeks. My birthday, which used to be our birthday. We never made a big deal out of it, yet we never spent one apart—until now.

With Greg sitting at the same table as me during lunch, I was entirely grateful for Matthew, Sarah, Mason, and *him* to join us.

Because I couldn't say a word to Greg.

Only an awkward, semi-forced hug—one I hadn't seen coming—before he said his good-bye.

Then, I retreated back to my room, crawling beneath the sheets, spending the rest of the day in bed, away from everyone.

If only I could hide from the pain.

Stuffing my face into my pillow, I attempt to fight off the onslaught of buried memories of my sister that rush to the surface. But, the harder I try, the more they invade my mind full force, my throat closing up while tears burn the backs of my eyes.

Slightly shifting my face to the darkened night sky of New York, I take another gasp when I hear someone entering my room.

Remaining utterly still, I wait for the person to go away.

"I know you're not sleeping," *he* says, his low voice reverberating throughout my body. "You're holding your breath."

*Rookie mistake.*

I push my face back into my pillow when I feel the bed dip down.

"Lauren"—his hand touches the small of my back—"look at me," he pleads instead of ordering me like he usually does.

I remain immovable even though he repeats my name in such a way that I know he won't let this go.

"I want to sleep—alone."

"You can do anything you want." Emphasizing my unlimited options, he finishes his sentence, "Except for that. I'm not leaving you."

*A night of crying in bed is off the table.*

Lifting my head, I ask him a question that'll make him regret every word he just said, "Anything?"

One word out of my mouth, and his eyes seem to darken already.

I wait for the moment when he corrects himself.

Yet he doesn't.

He just nods very slowly, wary of what's about to come.

"I want to go out."

He visibly relaxes, if only a little.

"And I want to get drunk," I state more firmly. "I'm twenty-one now. I'm legally allowed."

"No w—" he tries to object, but I don't let him finish.

"Anything!" Pause. "Your words!" Pause. "You give me that, or you leave me the hell alone."

He gets up from my bed and walks toward the window. A string of curses leave his mouth before he finishes with, "It's a bad idea, Lauren."

He's right. I'm not denying it. But he doesn't know how close I am to falling apart; it might be my only salvation to get through tonight.

"I won't leave you alone."

*Yeah, I got that part.*

"That means, you don't leave my side."

*Has he done something else in the past?*

"Being my girlfriend."

*What?*

"For the night."

I'm shaking my head in disbelief.

And yet, I'm considering joining a very dangerous game, one I should forfeit. But I can't. Not tonight when I've got much more to lose than my own values. My sanity is at stake here.

So, I give him the slightest nod.

"I mean it, Lauren. The moment you don't follow through on that, we're out of there."

I sigh as he comes up with another rule.

"And I don't want you wobbling on your feet. I don't care what the hell I initially said. I'm not risking your health."

"I can handle it," I assure him. *I've had a lot of practice.*

"Let's go," he orders, as if he wants to get it over with as fast as possible.

"Are you kidding me? I'm not going like this." I motion to my sweatpants.

"It's perfect." He nods.

"Out." I point at the door.

I rarely wear dresses, but on nights like this, I need to brighten up the outside to cover up the broken pieces on the inside. So, I pick out my deep blue dress I bought for Greg's niece's wedding. It's got a V-neck that dips quite low while my back is uncovered by a similar V-shape. A pair of short brown boots combined with a thin beige sweater, which can only be worn open, should be enough to give me some warmth to get to and from the club.

When I walk into the living room area with my new outfit and my hair hanging loosely from my shoulders, my eyes zero in on *him.* He's standing in the kitchen area, now wearing his black leather jacket.

While he takes in every inch of me, every curve that is now highlighted by my dress, I notice his rigid shoulders, his jaw clenching, as he slowly approaches me before he grabs the sides of my sweater, pulling them to get me closer to him.

Opening and closing his mouth, he finally says, "I'm not responsible for what happens to the idiots who stare at you tonight."

He hates the dress; I didn't expect differently. But for him to let it go so easily is as baffling as the fact that I'm flush against his body without the need to push him back.

Looking up into his eyes, I'm about to grace him with the first thank-you when the elevator dings.

*Company.*

I immediately take a step back, only to bounce back against his chest, as he's still holding on to my sweater.

Max, Mason, and Jaden enter the apartment, all dressed up, and they all set their eyes on me.

I expect a *gorgeous* comment from Mason, but he doesn't say a word, his mouth stretching into a thin line before he shifts his head toward *him*. "Is she going like that?"

As *he* shakes his head, his eyes warn Mason off.

"And, Max?" *He* pauses. "Get your eyes off my girlfriend, or you and I are going to have a problem."

*No. He. Didn't.*

My thankfulness evaporates into thin air while I slowly count to fifty, pretending he didn't just use the G-word for others to hear.

Letting go of my sweater, he gets out of his jacket before he holds it out to me. "Put this on."

"What?"

"Wear it."

Staring at his oversize jacket, I state the obvious, "It's huge." *And it doesn't match my dress. At. All.*

"I don't care. You're wearing it until we get inside."

"I won't do—"

"Then, the deal is off."

Eyes narrowed to thin slits, I know going back to bed with him next to me isn't an option. Snatching the jacket out of his hands, I slip both arms into it.

Mason and *he* look pleased at the sight of me.

*Idiots.*

We make it to The Qbe the same way as last time.

Only now, *he* joins me in the backseat of the Range Rover, his thigh connecting with mine while his left arm drapes along the top of the leather seat behind me.

And, when we walk toward the VIP area, he keeps a hand on my lower back the whole time.

He is there every step of the way, sticking to me like glue, heating my body in a way so that I can't tolerate his jacket a second longer once we are inside.

Halting in the middle of the hallway, I'm about to get it off when his fingers push harder into my lower back, urging me to keep on going.

"Leave it on."

"I'm freaking hot," I complain as *he* forces me to walk past the restrooms.

"Yeah, gorgeous, that's why you'd better leave it on," Mason explains, his arm brushing mine, as he's got my other side covered.

*Ugh.*

I make my strides bigger, keeping the damn jacket on, until we reach the lounge area where I shrug it off and throw it on the couch.

"Lauren?"

I turn around to face a stunned Sarah in a fine black dress.

"I thought you had a business dinner."

"We left since we got a phone call from Liam. He told us you changed your mind about celebrating your ..."

She doesn't say *the* word.

She knows I'm having a hard time dealing with all of it. Even though I convinced her these past few days that they shouldn't cancel their dinner for me, assuring her I wanted to be alone, she's here regardless.

"We didn't want to miss it."

I don't bother to stifle my smile.

"And what a beautiful dress you're wearing," she praises.

Matthew, standing a few feet away, talking to *him* and Mason, stops mid-sentence, hearing Sarah's words, his eyes inspecting my dress before he gives *him* a worried look.

*Yeah, I need a drink.*

Four cocktails later, I've already forgotten about *his* conditions or the brooding men around me. The dance floor is crowded, and the DJ is killing it. Matthew and Sarah are swinging on the dance floor, but I'm still stuck on the couch since *he* didn't feel like joining them. *He's* too busy talking to Mason next to him and Jaden across from him.

If he thinks I came out here to sit on a couch and get myself drunk, he's delusional.

*I need to dance.*

Subtly letting my napkin fall to the floor, I reach out to pick it up, ending up on all fours on the floor. With my body partly hidden by the high white cubical coffee table, I start crawling toward the exit of the lounge area.

*They'll never notice.*

"What are you doing?" *he* barks.

Hunched forward, I notice a pair of dark shoes one foot away from my hands.

*Busted.*

I ungraciously get to my full height, arms wide, as I try my best to keep my balance.

*No wobbling, Lauren.*

I consider five messed up lies, but only the truth pops out of my mouth. "I'm going to dance." He's about to say something, but I beat him to it. "Don't worry, baby." *Did I really just say that?* "You can dance with me," I assure him.

I haven't forgotten about our deal. Plus, the alcohol has consumed my body and mind. Right now, I would do quite anything to get on that dance floor.

Hesitating, he scans the crowd before he turns around, sighs, and grabs ahold of my hand. "Let's go." Dragging me along, he halts somewhere on the edge of the crowd. "Here," he stresses.

"I'd rather dance on our coffee table," I tease, the thundercloud above me not so happy about that suggestion.

With our hands still connected, I decide to try to take the lead, tugging at his hand. Instead of moving forward, I end up bouncing back against his chest.

*Screw him and all his muscle.*

"What are you doing, Lauren?"

*Working out?*

But I'd rather do it while dancing instead of using all my muscles to make him move.

"Follow me," I order as I pull one more time with the same result. A wave of disappointment washes over me when I look up into his eyes, and a, "Please," slips out of my mouth.

He shifts his gaze upward, gazing at the ceiling, as if he's asking for help from above, before he focuses his scolding dark eyes back on me.

Hoping God gave him the right advice, I try once more. This time, he actually follows, tightening his hold on my hand, while I search for a spot where we're completely surrounded by people.

The perfect spot to get lost in the music.

The perfect way to show Mr. Moody that there's more to life than his bubble of control.

With him scanning the crowd around us, switching our positions every time someone tends to come too close, I'm aware of the uneasy task, yet I'm determined to get rid of his tenseness as I sway my hips. My arms reaching over his shoulders, I intertwine my fingers behind his neck while I pull him close, demanding all his attention.

I've done this many times before. Yet I shouldn't be doing this with him.

Not with the guy who vowed he wouldn't stay away any longer.

Not with the guy who makes me glow inside and out.

I shouldn't.

But I am.

I'm thoroughly buzzed, my wall dissolving, as I feel his hands sliding down my waist and over my hips. His chocolate-brown eyes beam down at me, his body slowly thawing to mine, while the people around us fade to the background.

For once, we feel compatible.

Two unfitting pieces molding together to the beats of the music.

Revealing a whole other person.

A whole different *Liam*.

One who holds me without the need to control.

One whose focus is entirely on me instead of the possible threats out there.

One who dares to cup my butt while his mouth touches my lips.

A soft peck before his tongue demands entrance, before we start devouring one another, as if it were the last thing we'd do. A kiss so passionate that forever wouldn't be long enough.

Breaking it off is almost unbearable as I'm left light-headed and hungry for more. But he's back in control, keeping a small distance, as we move to the rhythm of the music.

We're in sync.

Together in a giant bubble.

Until it bursts.

Until I recognize that specific look.

*His* dark brown eyes alter to black while they narrow to thin slits, filled with a mix of emotions, focused on one thing.

My mouth runs dry, my hands quivering at the sight of him, at the realization that he's got *the* look. And it's not directed at me. It's on someone behind me.

Although every cell in my mind screams to let it go, my body is already turning around, zoning in on the person who I have to share that look with, who I have to burn to the ground for ruining this moment.

A tall girl with long, curly dark brown hair and a white slutty dress is leaning up against the bar. She looks about my age, maybe a little younger, but I can't deny that she's stunning.

Suppressing the sudden urge to walk up to her, grab a drink from the counter, and pour it all over her perfectly styled hair and model-worthy body, I barely keep it together when his hand clasps around my arm, pulling me with him. My boots refuse to cooperate with the sudden move, and that's the reason I misplace my foot, a sharp pain tearing through my ankle.

He doesn't notice—or he doesn't care—while I can do nothing but stumble behind him.

"Don't leave her out of your sight," *he* clips when we arrive in our lounge area. He presses me onto the couch in between Mason and Max.

My body complies, and my ankle hurts, but the dagger sticking into my back is what's killing me.

He's about to leave when he turns around, looking me over once more before he sets his eyes on Mason.

"And don't let her dance," *he* barks before he purposely strides away from us.

I'm left behind, stunned.

The places he touched when he dragged me here are blistered.

The way he just got rid of me is a hard slap in the face.

I wouldn't be Lauren Miller if I didn't pull the dagger out of my back and use it as a weapon to fight back.

Pulling off my boots, I push myself up, standing on two feet even though my left one hurts.

"I want to leave." There's no point in staying if I'm not allowed to dance, and I refuse to sit around and wait until he's had enough of his ex or girlfriend or whatever the hell she is.

I refuse to be his fallback.

I won't.

Mason is about to open his mouth when I deflect my gaze to Max. "You can't force me to stay," I point out.

Max exchanges glances with Mason while I grab my boots and step away from the bench.

"We'll go," Mason clips, blocking my exit with his body.

*Smart decision.*

Unless he wanted to physically hold me for the rest of the night.

"Put this on." He holds out his blazer.

I slip into it without any objection, as I would do quite anything to get out of this place.

We exit the VIP area.

But not before my eyes find *him* in the crowd.

His back facing me.

Two female arms are curled around his body.

My feet can't make it to the door fast enough—the sting of my ankle nearly forgotten—while Mason and Max flank my sides.

Mason even manages to arrange our pickup while walking. Because, when we leave the building, the black Range Rover is already in front of the back door, engine running with Bryan at the wheel.

For once, I welcome their precautions, grateful for their efficiency as I slide onto the backseat while I pull Mason's blazer tighter around me.

Not a word is spoken in the car or the elevator or once I'm back up in my room.

Silence so loud that it's deafening.

As much as I want to hate *him* or her, I can only hate myself for letting it get too far.

For not being indifferent.

For not being cold to his touch.

When in fact I'm a sizzling fire, trying to burn the image of them together.

Doing everything I wanted.

Everything I expected to happen.

I get in bed with my dress on, Mason lingering in the background, unsure of what to do.

I don't blame him. I'm screwed up.

As much as I want to fall into darkness, it doesn't work.

You can't put out a fire when every attempt provides extra oxygen, stirring it up.

Until I'm blazing.

Until the moment the bed dips down.

Until I recognize *his* voice.

Feel his soothing touch.

Smell his cologne.

And I ignite.

Flames lashing out.

How I want him to blister, but I can barely make him flinch.

Unable to land a solid punch on his muscled body.

Stabbed and bruised, I rip myself away from him and get out of bed, retreating.

My blue dress is rumpled, my hair a mess, the spitting image of the way I feel.

"Lauren."

I'm wavering—physically, emotionally. I hate this feeling even more than I hate him.

"I can explain."

I almost choke on the cliché of that one. I really don't need him to do anything but get the hell out of my face. If only I could shout it to his face, but words seem to fail me right now. I can only pray that my murderous glare gets the message across.

Yet our wishes are like us.

Always on opposite sides.

Every step he takes in my direction equals someone pushing on my chest a little harder. Up to the point where he's right in my personal space.

Towering over me.

Suffocating me.

"You're jealous," he whispers as he boxes me in between him and the wall, brushing a strand of hair out of my face.

I keep my eyes focused on his shirt, denying his words. Jealousy is reserved for lovers, which we're *absolutely* not. I'm merely disappointed that he discarded me as if I were trash.

He lifts my chin, our eyes connecting. "It's good to know." He smiles, and a dimple in his cheek is formed.

Seeing him overjoyed about it, I pull back, my eyes targeting the door, my way out.

"She's my sister," he speaks up.

I shift my eyes back to him, barely able to register his words as one hand cups my chin, his finger brushing along my lower lip right before his mouth connects with mine.

A soft kiss.

A small tug at my lower lip, and he repeats it one more time before adding, "If you don't believe it, ask Mason or Matthew."

*His sister.*

My brain is fried.

My senses heightened.

All my values are burned to ashes as I slant my mouth on his, rougher than we've done before, and every part of his body connects with mine.

Yet, somehow, it's still not close enough.

His hands sliding along my back, he cups my butt before he picks me up, and I wrap my arms and legs around him, my dress hitching up at the sudden movement.

As our lips keep meeting, he manages to walk across the room to take a seat on the bed with me in his lap.

And still, I want more.

I want to touch every inch of him.

Tugging at the hem of his shirt, I pull it up, and he cooperates, lifting his arms. Our kiss is shortly interrupted as I pull his shirt over his head and fling it across the room.

I reach out for the band of his jeans, fidgeting with his button, when he grabs my hands.

"Lauren, I don't think that's a good idea right now."

I look up at him with alarmed eyes, wondering how the hell he can think. I know I can't.

Still, he keeps my grabby hands restrained while he explains, "Don't get me wrong. I want this." His thumb starts drawing circles on the backs of my hands, soothing me. "But I want it all. I want all of you," he says, his eyes a darker shade.

All those times he crawled into my bed or claimed he wanted me, and now, all of a sudden, he wants to overthink this.

I can't.

Not with him half-naked in front of me.

The only answer I can give him is by slamming a kiss on his mouth.

Just for a second.

Before he breaks it off again.

Reluctantly.

He's caving in. I can feel it.

Leaning his forehead against mine, he sighs, "Just tell me you'll try to give us a shot."

*Try. Oh, I love that word, the freedom that comes with it.*

I nod eagerly as I try to catch another kiss.

162

"Tell me," he urges on as he leans back, his lips out of reach.

I look him in the eye, ready to say about anything to get what I want, but instead, I use my words wisely, as I refuse to lie. "I'll try."

I'll try. And fail. I'm my mother's daughter after all.

Yet, right here and now, that's enough for him to go through with this.

He lets go of my hands and reaches out for the hem of my dress, slowly pulling it over my head.

With a dark glint in his eye—unmistakable and impossible to ignore—he finally has me in my black underwear, in his lap, straddling him.

Burying my hands in his hair, I snatch another kiss as he picks me back up, laying me onto the bed, the softness of the blanket caressing my back.

He's on top, in full control.

All my values, nothing but dust.

In this moment, I'm totally lost as to why I would even bother having him above me. I can only focus on his mouth, on his body, all too eager to get rid of his remaining clothes.

I'm rushing this.

Grasping this moment of insanity with both hands.

Before the million reasons I shouldn't be doing this infiltrate my mind and ruin it all.

His approach is—to no surprise—the exact opposite.

He's doing anything and everything to prolong this moment, placing kisses all over my body, teasing me until I almost come undone.

"Liam," I breathe, his name on my lips for the second time—only, this time, anger isn't surging through my veins.

I endure his torture.

I let him remove my bra and panties in such a slow and vulnerable way; it's almost unbearable.

To top it all, he pushes up and away from me, leaving me completely naked as he pulls something out of his wallet.

A condom.

God, how I feel so much like the guy right now, not even thinking about taking precautions. I can only grasp on to the blankets as he strips off his jeans and boxers.

The anticipation almost ripping me to pieces.

But then he's back, arching above me as he hovers, his dark eyes beaming before he slowly slips inside me.

And I experience everything as if I were a virgin with the way he's treating me.

Fragile.

Unique.

With every thrust, he keeps his eyes set on mine, as if he were looking straight into my soul.

It's too intense, how he's claiming my body and mind.

Too close, how he's taking over.

But, when I shut my eyes, he halts, forcing me to acknowledge *this. Us*.

So, I do.

I give him my eyes.

No more wall.

No more holding back.

My eyes command him to pick up the pace.

As I want all of him.

Seeing I'm not holding back any longer, he moves faster. Harder.

Until the edge is close, and I can't do anything but cling to him as I sail beyond, groaning, waiting when he reaches his climax.

We both end up panting, holding on to each other, and then Liam rolls onto his back, taking me with him, as he refuses to let me go.

Such a vulnerable position, my head on his chest, the erratic pounding of his heart evident proof of what just happened.

But, right in this moment, I'm like him, treasuring every second.

Without any regret.

Without any fear.

While my conscience is banging on the door.

It's closed.

For now.

Only a matter of time before it takes back the upper hand.

Before it encourages me to run away.
From the only thing that's ever felt this good.

# CHAPTER 34
## LAUREN

Walking through the hallway of SPISe's Critical Response Department, a major smile plastered on my face, I enjoy the fact that there's no elephant haunting me in every room. All of it is because *he* is out of town.

Ever since our passionate night, he's been pushing whatever this is even further, reminding me of my promise to give *us* a chance.

And I did. In that moment, I gave myself completely. The day afterward was awful, as I dealt with my relentless conscience and *him,* overbearing and extremely frustrated.

It was absolutely exhausting, how I had to fight both him and myself.

But, today, I woke up happy, relieved to get my much-needed breathing space. A sharp contrast to *his* behavior, as he had acted like a complete basket case because he had to go on a business trip with Matthew. Away from me. If it wasn't for Matthew insisting, he would have canceled.

"Mason will handle it," Matthew had assured.

Basically saying, he would handle *me,* if there was really a need to handle anything in the first place, as we'd been ordered to stay in.

I'm just helping out Sarah with work while Max—not Mason since he was called away by Dean—lingers in the background.

"Lauren, could you take this to Sebastian for me?" Sarah asks, stuffing a folder into my hands.

"Sure. Where can I find him?"

She gives me directions, and I'm off down the hall, searching for Sebastian's office.

Another quick errand, a job that keeps my troubled mind occupied.

Returning from Sebastian's office, I decide to use the restroom first.

Locking myself into a stall, I hear someone else entering while I finish up.

As I get out, I stumble into someone, a male someone, and he's right in front of me, as if he's been waiting for me to come out.

"Max?" I look up at him, taking in his features, how he's more imposing than I've ever seen him. "Is something wrong?"

He fidgets with something in his hand.

"What is it?" I press.

He looks up at me while his fingers squeeze his phone a little harder. "There's something I want you to see."

Unsure of what he could be so stressed about, I nod reassuringly. "Sure." I have no clue what to expect or what could possibly be so bad for me to see.

"Okay. But I need for you to act fast and do exactly as I say."

I give him a wary look as he slams his backpack on the floor in between us, and alarm bells start to ring in my head.

Shifting my eyes to the door, I notice something black sticking at the bottom of it, something that's clearly blocking the door from opening.

*This is definitely not good.*

"You can trust me."

*Says the rapist to his victim.*

"We don't have much time," he stresses as he holds out his cell phone. "Just press play."

While he keeps a distance, I take his phone and press the play button. The screen fills up with a girl sitting front and center on a couch, holding out a yellow Post-it note. The one I got from Sarah about a week ago—a message lying on the breakfast table, wishing me a wonderful day with an added funny smiley face to the side of her text.

It's weird to see it in this video. But that's not the reason my heart is missing a beat or three.

Or why my breath is stuck down my throat.

It's the fact that the girl holding my sticky note is my sister, alive and well, her hazel eyes staring right back at me.

"How?" I whisper, dumbfounded, while I listen to my sister's angelic voice.

"Lauren, sis, I'm alive. I know it's hard to believe, and I would love to explain everything, but you don't have much time. Just listen to Max, go with him, and we'll be together soon."

I gawk at the screen as another person walks into the picture. He plops down onto the couch next to my sister, his face becoming visible.

"I'm with Dad," Kate continues. "He has been taking care of me. Now, move your butt and come home," she says.

Tears well in the corners of my eyes as the video ends.

I press play one more time, wanting to see her again, analyze every detail, memorize every move I never thought I'd see again.

"There's no time for this. Or any explanation," Max snaps, snatching the phone out of my hands. "We have to move before someone notices you've been gone too long. Before they start looking for you."

"I don't understand." I shake my head as the most evident question pops out. "How do I know this is not a trap?" The video could be fake, all of it a lie, a serious attempt to kill me, too.

"You don't. It's all I've got. It's all I can give you. You need to decide now. You change into these clothes I've brought"—he motions to the backpack—"and walk out of this building with me. Or you can stay here, and I'll leave." He pauses. "For good."

I'm still stunned, frozen in place. Then again, I don't need to consider my options; it's an obvious choice even though every cell in my body screams to consider the other. Yet I would make a deal with the devil to get a chance at seeing my sister again.

"What do I need to wear?"

A blonde wig, glasses, classy black pants, a white shirt, and a dark blazer. The whole outfit is nothing I would normally wear, but that's exactly the point.

Changing clothes, I come back out of a stall, handing Max my old clothes. He stuffs them in his backpack before he throws it into one of the other stalls.

"Go straight to the elevator. I'll be right behind you. We'll take the elevator to the basement and take my car from there. Don't speak to anybody, and if somebody talks to you, I'll jump in," he explains.

One nod is enough confirmation for him to remove the object obstructing the door and leave.

My heart rate is beyond normal, and my breath is erratic as I walk through the hallway, my eyes fixed on the elevator. I smother the deep, dark voice in my head demanding me to stop, turn around, and run away from Max.

I can't listen to it, as I can't think about anything but my sister, alive, smiling, waiting for me. It's enough reason for me to get into the elevator and follow Max to his car before I slip into the black BMW. All without any problems.

"I need your bracelet," Max demands as he sits behind the wheel.

"What?"

My silver bracelet, the one I've never taken off since I got it from my sister.

"No way."

"It's got a tracker."

"That's not possible. I never—"

"You did. When you were at the hospital, they removed it, installed a tracker, and put it back."

"What?"

"Look, you can either give it to me or get out of the car. Because there's no point in leaving with you wearing it," Max says as he holds out his hand.

My mouth opens, but no words come out.

"Lauren," he pushes, losing his patience.

I reluctantly pull it off my arm and push it into his hand.

"Anything else? Do you need to cut me somewhere?"

"This isn't the movies, Lauren," he says as he throws my bracelet out the window. "Now, let's get the hell out of here," he says, reversing the car and speeding out of the garage.

Away from SPISe.

And hopefully toward my sister.

Something I've wanted for so long and someone I would've moved heaven and earth just to see once again.

Yet running has never felt this wrong.

# CHAPTER 35
## VANCE

*A Year and Three Months Ago*

"Max, can you come in here for a second?" I wave for him to step into my office and take a seat as I position myself behind my desk. "I've got a proposition for you."

Looking up at me, he remains unfazed. He's only twenty-two, and already, he's more qualified than some who've been in the business for over ten years.

"I need you to apply for a job at Scotts' Private Investigation and Security in New York."

"What?"

"Don't get me wrong; I think you're an asset to our team. That's why I need you to apply. It's a personal favor, one I can't explain. Not right now. I just need for you to get the job and work your way up because I need to know everything Matthew Scott is working on."

Including the job I've hired him to do, the one he accepted on one condition—that I had to let him handle it.

No updates.

No communication unless there's an emergency.

A condition I've agreed to. But that doesn't mean I can't get the information somewhere else. Or from someone else.

Since I know Matthew just sent his most loyal employee—his brother—across the country, Max is an excellent replacement for Mason. And the perfect guy for me to have on the inside.

"You'll get paid by him. And me."

"I'll do it." He nods.

I know he's not only in it for the money. The guy loves a challenge, doesn't have a girlfriend or close family, and likes to explore the world. Getting paid double is just a nice benefit for him.

"Thanks," I say as I get up and walk over toward him. "Now, go pack your bag. Your flight leaves at four p.m."

Max gets up from his chair, grinning, unbothered that I've already booked his flight because I knew he would take the job.

Clasping a hand around his shoulder, I tell him, "Go and work your ass off."

*I'm counting on you.*

# CHAPTER 36
## LIAM

*Present*

I had a bad feeling from the moment I opened my eyes and saw Lauren lying beside me.

How she cracked a smile, the first real one in three days, when she knew I was about to leave.

If only I could stay.

But Lauren's father had insisted on meeting Matthew *and* me today.

Knowing what he could do and how he could endanger Lauren, we had to meet his demands. But not without using the opportunity for our own benefit.

And we did.

Although he seemed ticked off about something. And, based on the murderous glances he shot my way, I had something to do with it.

Yet I couldn't care less.

I just needed to send him a message.

Unable to hide my cocky attitude or my asshole remarks, I was there to dump his shitload of dumb decisions right in front of him and shove it in his face. Everything to make him see that he had to let Lauren go. I wouldn't let him ruin her life, too; he'd have to crawl over my cold and lifeless body to do so.

Regardless of the venom in his eyes, the hate he sent my way, hearing me remind him of everything, he knew I was right.

The guilt that had surely made a giant hollowness inside his chest—one that'd been filled with remorse, bitterness, and most of all, pain—forced him to make the right decision.

As I drive us back home, I'm satisfied our trip wasn't in vain, but I seem to be the only one since Matthew has been tight-lipped from the moment we got into the car.

He's a straightforward guy. The fact that he's keeping it to himself makes it irrelevant for me, probably work-related.

"She's in the meeting room," Matthew clips as we enter the elevator, and he jabs the corresponding button. I shoot him a questioning look, and I get an immediate answer, "Lauren is helping Sarah with some paperwork."

*I know that. She's fine.*

I called Mason, who put Max, of all people, through.

Apparently, Dean had a problem with a client, needing Mason's immediate assistance. Max was the only one hanging around, the only person who could keep an eye on her and put her through when I wanted to hear her voice.

Although she couldn't take the phone, I heard Lauren say, "Hey," from afar.

It was enough for me to flush my bad feeling down the drain, to drive back with some peace of mind.

That's how I walk into the meeting room, blindsided with lies because I only see Bryan, Jaden, and Sebastian.

No Max.

No Mason.

But, most of all, no Lauren.

And I know I've been foolish.

Absolutely stupid for smothering my gut feeling.

Unable to do anything but fixate all my regret and anger on the person I trusted, the person who was brooding on the way back here, busy returning texts on his cell phone.

He fucking knew.

"Where. Is. She?"

Jaden positions himself in front of the door while Bryan and Sebastian step a little closer toward me. It's obvious that they're all expecting for me to lose it. Ironic how they've put me in the same meeting room where Lauren lost it a few months ago. Only, now, the glass table has been replaced with a solid and very much unbreakable white table, making it the perfect room to go mad in.

"Sit down," Matthew orders. "I'll explain."

If he thinks I'll be able to sit this one out, he really doesn't know me.

But, because he has the information and I want him to be physically able to tell me, I keep myself from stalking up to him and throwing a solid punch.

"Talk."

Matthew, the asshat who even took the time to prep this little meeting, walks up to the new touchscreen TV hanging from the wall to open up a video file. He presses play, and the only thing I can do is brace myself as I look at the video footage of a hallway that shows a woman with blonde hair, glasses, and a dress suit exiting the restroom and walking toward the elevator with Max on her tail.

"About three hours ago, Lauren entered the restroom. Max went in right after, and ten minutes later, they both exit with Lauren dressed as a blonde secretary. We found her clothes in a backpack in one of the stalls." He pauses, looking me in the eye, before he continues, "No sign of struggle."

*No. She. Didn't.* The video continues.

This time, it's footage of the basement, showing how they exited the elevator and walked up to a black BMW parked near it. Stepping closer to the screen, I watch her every move, how she willingly gets into his car and how they leave together before the screen goes black.

My hands, which have been curled into fists since the moment I realized it was her, slam against the wall. I let my head hang while I scream the only word that comes to mind, "Fuck!"

Which I am. Truly. Fucked.

I'm completely torn apart, seeing her willingly leave me behind after everything we shared.

After I finally got through to her.

After we started giving *us* a chance.

And then there's Max.

"I knew something was off about him!"

The fucker who played us all, the mole we were trying to flush, who'd better pray he'll never see me again if he wants to live and breathe another day. How I despise myself for trusting him with her, how I want to blame Matthew for his lack of screening his employee.

A lesson learned the hard way.

But I'm not giving up. I've been fighting for us for a while now.

She can run.

It's what she does best.

But she can't hide.

We've made sure of that.

"Her tracker," I speak up as I lift my head, a spark of hope to get her back. Fast.

"We found it in the basement. Max must have removed it." Matthew sighs, rubbing a hand over his face, showing I'm not the only one who's holding on by a thread.

The fucker knew. He planned all of it.

Cornering her in the restroom, giving her other clothes, parking a getaway car near the elevator, getting rid of her tracker.

He orchestrated the whole thing. And he had perfect timing.

"Max waited until we were gone to do this," I fume.

"Or someone else made sure we had a meeting, so Max could execute their plan," Matthew clues in.

"Vance?" I push away from the wall and stare at him, dumbfounded. "You think he's behind this?"

"Max deceived us all, but he left a trail. Every employee is forced to use our own secure cell phones. We searched his records and found a phone number of one of Vance's coworkers," he explains. "Since our little run-in in the park, Sebastian and I have been monitoring Vance, mapping out who's been working for him."

Matthew's professionalism doesn't disappoint, not totally. He might have misjudged Max for being a mole and Lauren for cooperating, but if he gets me Lauren back, I might forgive him.

"Have you contacted Vance?"

"We tried half an hour ago. He's incommunicado."

No coincidence.

The fact that he was so cooperative and didn't press the matter of getting Lauren back, it suddenly fits the picture.

"We'll find him," Matthew promises when he walks up to me, placing a hand on my shoulder. "We'll get her back," he vows.

I have no doubt.

We have to.

If it's the last thing I do.

# Chapter 37
## LAUREN

*Not the movies.*

Not when we ditch our car in the middle of nowhere to switch to another one, which Max knew exactly where to find and had the keys to.

Not when he picks up another guy who I'm sure is able to crush a rabbit with only one hand.

Not when I notice that they're each carrying a gun or that they've ordered me to slip into a bulletproof vest after I shrugged off my dark blazer—I got rid of my wig and glasses the moment we drove away.

*This isn't the movies, Lauren. Not. At. All.*

Well then, Max surely hasn't seen a lot of movies because this feels exactly like one. And it freaks me out.

I'm trapped in a car with Max and Mr. Rabbit, who tends to look at me every ten seconds to check if I'm still in the backseat of a moving car.

It's a miracle they haven't shot me already. Then again, they gave me a bulletproof vest, so at least they want to keep me alive. For now. Until we reach our destination, wherever that might be.

"We're almost there," Max explains, sitting next to me since Mr. Rabbit is the driver now.

I shift my gaze to him, taking in all his features, seeing how he's transformed into a whole other person since he approached me in the restroom.

Being around Matthew, Mason, and *him*, Max always seemed confident but not capable of handling such an operation on his own. But, now, I feel intimidated by him. He knows exactly what he's doing, and although I don't think he'll physically hurt me, I haven't been able to give him much lip. Although I might have caused some trouble when *he* called.

*"Shit. Liam's calling," Max said as his screen lit up.*

*We had barely left the building, and already, he was on to me.*

*"Talk to him. Tell him you're fine, that you're just running an errand for Sarah," he said as he held out the phone that was vibrating in his hand.*

*"You mean, lie to him?"*

*The guy has a sense of where I'm at without seeing me.*

*I couldn't talk to him; he'd know something was up after hearing one word.*

*"I can't do it."*

*"You have to," he barked, losing his temper. "He'll never be happy with just my word."*

*Point taken. But I knew, if I did talk to him, I would mess it all up.*

*"He'll know."*

*Max scrutinized me over before he pulled to a stop along the road and pushed the green button, holding the phone to his ear. "Liam." I heard him rambling before Max answered, "She's fine, running an errand for Sarah. I'm with her right now."*

*Silence.*

*Then, Max said, "I'll let you talk to her."*

*He held out the phone again, and I waved my arms, indicating that I couldn't take it.*

*He gave me a murderous look before he put the phone back to his ear. I heard his increasingly worried voice loud and clear.*

*"Yeah, Liam, I'm afraid she's got her hands full right now," Max said with bunched eyebrows as his voice rose another octave.*

*He was getting antsy.*

*"I'll hold it out to her," Max said again as he put the phone on speaker. He lipped the words, Say something.*

*So, I did. I yelled a chipper, "Hey," as I waved at the phone— or more like, waved at Max to wrap it up.*

*With him listening in, Max couldn't do much more than put it back to his ear.*

*"She's looking forward to seeing you again," he said while I swallowed down his lie.*

*That was when I realized, if all of this was a trap, worst-case scenario, I might never see him again, and I had just thrown away my last chance to talk to him.*

Shit.

*I motioned for Max, who was still on the phone, to hand it to me.*

*Shifting his head, he scrutinized my expression, and a frown creased his forehead.*

*"Safe drive home," he clipped to him before he ended the call. He pushed a button to open the window and threw his cell out onto the street. "We won't need that anymore."*


That's how I lost my chance at saying good-bye. Now, I can only brace for what's to come while we drive past a gate and down a long winding driveway as a little mansion comes into view.

It's the perfect murder scene; the houses are so far apart that the neighbors would never hear me scream.

"We've arrived," Mr. Rabbit says into the phone he's got pressed to his ear, disturbing my sick thoughts.

He nods in Max's direction, who in turn looks at me.

"Follow me," Max says before he gets out of the car and opens my door to let me out. He guides me up the few steps toward the house.

With Mr. Rabbit behind me and Max next to me, the only thing I can do is follow him into the house to see another man waiting.

*I've got a bad feeling about this.*

As I'm scanning the hallway for a possible way out, I hear someone calling my name.

Stuck in time and space, I look around me, surrounded by men while the voice I just heard was a female one.

But then it echoes one more time.

A soft, familiar voice that makes the hairs on my neck stand up.

*It can't be.*

My mind is playing tricks on me, but that doesn't stop my feet from walking toward the living room, in the direction where it came from.

I turn the corner and search the room, my heart pumping harder with every inch I scan.

I see someone sitting on the edge of the couch, a brunette with hazel eyes. Like mine.

My eyes can't believe what my mind is screaming.

*Kate.*

*She's here.*

*She's alive.*

I stagger back against the doorpost, the nightmare of her death invading my conscience, as I try to grasp what's right in front of me.

"Lauren," Kate speaks up, slowly rising from the couch, her voice so breakable, full of uncertainty.

It's enough for my legs to strengthen.

To be the Lauren I've always been around her.

The person she needs me to be.

Strong.

Reliable.

"Kate," I say with a regained solid voice, tears prickling in the corners of my eyes.

I push away from the door and walk in her direction when she starts moving toward me.

Slowly.

Until she ends up running the last few feet, and then we fall into each other's arms.

Holding on for dear life, she hugs the oxygen right out of my lungs as she starts to sob.

Her scent, her familiar touch, the memories still lingering in the back of my mind unleash something inside me.

I've made a habit of hiding my emotions, but now, I can't stop the tears from falling while I hold on to her as much as she holds on to me.

Until we run out of tears.

Until we're both convinced that this is really happening.

Until we've managed to smother our sobs to actually talk to each other.

"How is this possible?" I ask.

I've taken a small step back while I keep ahold of her hands, squeezing them to assure myself that this isn't some sort of hallucination.

"I got lucky." She sniffs, a smile appearing on her face.

I smile back, hearing those words, the same ones the doctors once told me.

"I almost bled to death. If it wasn't for the quick and correct assistance, I wouldn't have made it." She swallows. "I owe my life to *him*," she finishes, leaving out *his* name on purpose. For me.

My heart swells in my chest.

And I smile even brighter.

Silently thanking Liam.

For being *him*.

So.

Freaking.

Stubborn.

# Chapter 38
## LIAM

It's been fifteen hours since her disappearance.

Every single minute has been spent on helping the team find her, on contacting Vance.

Nothing so far.

I'm losing my goddamn mind, and I'm not the only one. Mason's all over the place. He wasn't with me when they explained Lauren's disappearance because he was too busy tearing another room apart. I saw him shortly after. How the guilt was ripping him to pieces.

He was here when she slipped right under his nose, making it that much harder to work through this failure.

Our failure.

We're all to blame. We all made the mistake of trusting Max.

And Lauren.

"Shouldn't you get some sleep?" Matthew asks as he walks into the Operations Control Room—or the OCR, as we tend to call it.

"We haven't found her," I state while I stare at Sean's screen—our IT guy, who's an expert at tracking down people—with Max's phone records on display.

"That's exactly why you should go to bed. You can't focus when you're sleep-deprived. We need you," he points out.

I realize it's necessary to have a clear mind, and I know the whole team is doing overtime.

Still, going to bed is pointless.

I'll never be able to sleep without her, knowing she's out there. Alone.

"I'll sleep when I have her back," I reply as I look back at the screen.

I won't stop.

Not until she's back in my arms.

Where she belongs.

# Chapter 39
## LAUREN

Waking up to see my sister lying next to me, alive and very much snoring, I feel like the luckiest girl on the planet.

Chatting until late last night, we went to bed together, as if almost nothing had changed. Only a different house, a king-size bed, and a slim chance at falling out of it.

It's still unbelievable, how our lives were ripped apart.

How I was grieving her death while she was struggling to stay alive after getting shot. They even had to keep her in a coma for two days to keep her from having excruciating pain. After that, she still had a hard recovery, mainly fighting numerous infections and getting physical therapy on a daily basis to regain her strength.

With Kate being so openhearted about everything, I decided to keep my side of the story to myself—at least, for now. I don't want to bother her with my ridiculous issues in comparison to hers.

And I'm definitely not ready to explain how the guy who I used to refuse to call by name became the guy who's been sleeping in my bed. And then some.

Regardless, I can't bring myself to talk about Liam, not after my little escapade with Max, how I left him without so much as a word.

"What's wrong?"

Shaking my head, I look down on my sister. "I thought you were sleeping," I say, a little astonished.

"Yeah, well, you're a loud thinker." She sighs, pushing her back up against the headboard, so she's sitting right next to me. "Something you want to talk about?"

"Not really."

Kate's probably the only person who knows not to push any further.

Throwing the blankets off her, she swings her legs out of bed. "Fair warning, Dad will come and visit us today," she says before she saunters toward the bathroom.

She's already in the Dad phase while I'm still trying to handle my murderous thoughts involving him.

"He wasn't here yesterday because he wanted to give us some time alone," she goes on, rummaging in the bathroom with the door open.

Sighing, I slide back down under the covers, a sudden need to stay in bed all day.

"Lauren, you have to give him a chance. He's been taking great care of me. He faked my death, so I wouldn't be in danger anymore," she pleads, coming out of the bathroom with her toothbrush in hand.

*He could've told me. Spared me from suffering for months.*

"He brought us back together."

*By kidnapping me. And why does he care so much now when he never wanted us before?*

"Don't worry. He won't stay very long. He's too busy finding the man who tried to kill me. Us."

*Maybe he should do that and only that.*

But I keep it all to myself until we're both freshened up, fully clothed—because we're surely not alone in this house—and sitting at the breakfast table when Vance walks in, giving Kate a kiss on the top of her head.

"Hi, Dad," she says as she stands up and wraps her arms around him.

Only when Kate is sitting back down do I notice how Vance's eyes dare to look my way.

Only then do I feel how the need to get straight answers trumps the fact that my sister is not going to like this conversation. Yet it's my undying love for her that forces me to give him the third degree. She was heartbroken when we lost our mother. I can't stand by and watch her go through that again.

"Did Max treat you right during the trip?" he asks, leaning slightly against the counter behind him.

I look him straight in the eye as I demand, "Maybe you should start by explaining to me who Max really is."

*He sure as hell isn't Matthew's loyal employee. Not anymore.*

"That's not important."

"Yes, it is!" I exclaim, pushing away my bowl before I get up and away from my chair, turning my back to him. I'd love to push the subject, but not with Kate as my audience. And not before I've made an important demand. "I need to call SPISe."

"You're not calling them," he snaps. "We're done."

"Done?" I ask, turning around to face him. "You've lured me out of their building without any explanation, and that's how you're going to leave it?"

"Yes."

"What—"

"I asked nicely in the park. And I called Matthew twice to arrange a meeting with you, which he both declined. I was done asking." He pauses. "You're my daughter. I shouldn't have to ask in the first place."

"I'm not your daughter," I fire back.

"Lauren," Kate pleads, a pained expression on her face.

Yet I keep my focus on Vance, I'm not ready to let this go. I have to let *them* know I'm okay; it can't end this way.

"If you want to earn my trust, you'll have to give me answers. And you'll have to let me call SPISe. They've taken care of me—"

"A little too well."

"What's that supposed to mean?"

"It means that they were supposed to keep you safe. Not set you up with a guy who hooks up with you," he hisses.

"How did you—" I gasp when realization sets in. "Max."

"Thank God for him. I knew I needed an inside man. The moment I heard you were sleeping with William Drew fucking Ressler, I was done."

*William?*

"He would've kept taking advantage of you to get you under his control when he should have been doing his goddamn job. That's what I pay him for."

*Pay him for?*

I waver on my feet, my hands digging into the chair in front of me.

Even though I'm still standing upright, it feels as if I was just tackled to the ground, forced to see another perspective, one that makes me sick to my stomach.

*"Stay with a friend of mine."* Those were Greg's words.

*"We'll take care of Lauren."* Matthew's words.

*Was all of it a lie? Was I just a job he had to do?*

"Lauren."

*Every word he said.*

*Every single touch.*

*Every kiss.*

*All of it fake?*

*A way to keep me in line?*

"Look, it doesn't matter. I would've gotten you out of there regardless. I wanted you two to be together. I just waited until Kate was better and until I had a safe place for the both of you."

I've changed my focus to the table instead of him. "I need to go."

And so I bolt out of the kitchen and toward the front door, desperate for some fresh air. I'm about ten feet away from the door when one of my dad's employees crosses my path, forcing me to halt in the middle of the hallway.

"You can't just run out the door, Lauren. It's safe inside this house. Not out there," Vance explains, his strained voice coming from behind me.

I felt like the luckiest girl this morning, but now, I feel goddamn awful, my chest rising and falling heavily. If I don't do something fast, I'll have an anxiety attack in Vance's presence.

With my back still facing him, I hiss, "I'm going to bed."

I run up the stairs and into my room before I throw myself onto the bed, stuffing my face into my pillow when someone enters the room.

“Lauren,” Kate urges, the bed dipping down as her hand lands on my shoulder. “Talk to me.”

I shift my head the other way, taking deep breaths in and out.

“Lauren?” The quiver in her voice is undeniable.

She’s probably freaking out since I’ve never had this kind of anxiety attack around her.

“I’m fine,” I whisper.

She doesn’t say another word.

Instead, she gets into bed next to me, her body pressing against my side, her arm across my back.

Holding on to me.

As I fall apart.

# Chapter 40
## LIAM

Three days without a single sign of life, without a clue as to her whereabouts.

Without her.

An incoming call drags my knuckles away from the punching bag in front of me.

Droplets of sweat falling to the ground, I hold my breath as I accept the call from an unknown number.

"I need your help."

Not the soft, sweet voice I craved to hear, but the voice of the guy who should replace the punching bag in front of me.

*Max.*

"You fucker!" I scream as my taped hand connects with the bag one more time.

Before I'm able to breathe through my anger.

Before I can focus on his words.

"You'd better start talking—"

"I thought that it was safe enough to do it this way. That Vance had it all handled. I would've never—"

Anger rippling along my skin, I scream so loud that every single person in the fitness room sets their eyes on me, including Mason, the only one who dares to move in my direction.

"Where the hell is she?"

"I'll text you our location." He pauses. "Get SPISe on it. I want them out of here—sooner rather than later."

*Them?*

"What the fuck are you saying?"

"Just hurry," he says before he disconnects.

I get an encrypted text, a code SPISe uses.

Squeezing my phone hard, I take in his full message before I clasp on to Mason's shoulder, shoving my cell phone in his face.

Max's text has a location and a clear message.

*The dead have resurrected.*

*Get Lauren and Kate out of here ASAP.*

# Chapter 41
## LAUREN

Vance is gone.

But he couldn't leave without another word with me alone.

*"Matthew doesn't know."*

*"What?"*

*"Nobody knows that Kate's alive. Not even Greg." He sighed. "I didn't just lie to you. I also lied to them. That's the reason you can't call SPISe. I can't have you talking to them about her. The fewer people know, the better. Calvetti won't look for a girl who's already dead."*

*I shook my head in disbelief.*

*"Besides, they know you're with me, that you're safe."*

*"So, that's it then? I can't call them, and I can't go out."*

*"You can leave, but you'll have to live with the risks of doing so. You have to know that you'll endanger both Kate and yourself by doing that."*

*"So, we'll have to live like this for ..."*

*"As long as it takes to get the situation under control."*

There are too many unknowns, lots of unanswered questions, and there's nothing I can do about it.

"Something's different," Kate says out of the blue.

We're on the couch, on opposite ends with a bowl of popcorn in between us while *The Hunger Games* is playing on TV. It's day four of our stay here, and I'm doing everything I can to distract my anxious mind.

"What are you talking about?" I ask, stuffing popcorn into my mouth, chewing it like gum, as I'm not hungry at all.

"You've changed," she says, a wary look on her face.

Shrugging it off, I know she's right, yet I hope she'll let it go.

"Do you miss *him?* Dad didn't tell me a lot about you. I knew you were somewhere safe. But not where and not with who—"

Tearing my eyes away from the screen, I look her straight in the eye. "I ..." But I can't finish my sentence. I can't lie to her.

After everything Vance has told me, I'm not ready to get into this subject. Even with her.

And I don't get a chance either as a deafening boom echoes through the house.

A bang so loud that I know something is terribly wrong.

Completely stunned, I stare in the direction of the noise while Max does the complete opposite.

Appearing out of thin air, he gets me off the couch and in his arms before he forces me to crouch down and pushes me toward the kitchen.

And yet, my only concern isn't in my line of vision.

*Kate.*

As much as I can fight Max's muscles, I hold back as I try to turn us around to see my sister in the arms of Levi—my father's employee, who's been assigned to Kate from when she was still in the hospital—ready to follow us out. It's enough reassurance for me to cooperate and let Max do his job, herding us out of there.

As if they've been training for this every day, we reach the back door in record time where Mr. Rabbit is waiting, motioning for us to leave the house.

Night has fallen, so we can't see very far ahead, but that doesn't stop them from moving forward at a fast pace, crossing the lawn.

I follow Max's every move. I'm not stupid. I heard the explosion; that didn't sound like someone who wanted to say hello. I can only hope we're actually going somewhere safe, that they're getting Kate somewhere safe.

Running across the long yet narrow yard, I now notice how the house is located in between two streets and how we're headed to the street at the back of the house.

Relief washes over me when we're about to exit the yard. But the thought alone jinxes the whole operation as I notice movement in my peripheral vision.

Instead of moving forward, Max freezes.

Pulling my back against his chest, he slightly shifts his body, so it partly shields mine before he outstretches his arm, a gun in hand, while I gape at the scene unfolding around us.

*This is not happening.*

I didn't have the average life. It was filled with scenes that most people couldn't cope with. I handled it because I was always prepared for the worst.

But I never prepped myself for explosions, for getaways late at night, for men with guns.

For *this.*

My eyes slide to every person scattered across the yard. We're at a complete standstill, fenced in by *him*, Mason, Matthew, Jaden, Colin, and Dean, all wearing a no-nonsense look.

*What the hell are they doing?*

"Get your hands off her!" *his* voice roars through the night air, demanding Max's attention, which he gains immediately.

*His* deathly stare with eyes the darkest shade of brown, a weapon in hand, his body in full defensive mode, he claims everyone's attention. Including Mr. Rabbit and another man, who've joined us.

"Let them go!" Mason booms, both hands on his Glock, his arms strained, as he refers to both Kate and myself.

Looking to my right side, I see how Levi is holding Kate in a similar way. How we're out in the open, surrounded by narrow-minded, testosterone-filled men who have no regard for my sister, who's struggling to hold it together.

Too many guns.

Too many reminders.

I need to stop this nonsense. I just don't have a clue how.

"We need to talk," Matthew interjects.

*Only men try to organize a meeting by wielding their guns.*

"Vance is done working with you," Mr. Rabbit speaks up.

"We've got a proposition. But, first, let's move to another location. We're out in the open, and our little diversion caused a lot of noise," Matthew admits, holstering his gun.

*They did this?*

"We're handling it," Mr. Rabbit interjects. "We don't need your help."

"Yes, you're handling it perfectly," *he* fumes, taking a step closer.

"The fact that we found you is enough reason for you to hear us out," Matthew points out, mirroring *his* moves.

Mr. Rabbit exchanges looks with both Max and Levi before he sets his eyes back on Matthew and lowers his gun. "Fine. You've got ten minutes. We'll follow you." He motions to the parked SUV.

They're all busy holstering their guns.

But *his* gun is still aimed at Max.

Matthew is the only one who dares to push it to the ground, suggesting, "Let's go."

No more guns pointed in my direction, I slip out of Max's hold, avoiding eye contact with *him* as I walk straight toward my sister, pulling her out of Levi's arms and into mine.

Hugging her close to my chest, I squeeze my eyes closed when I hear some commotion behind me.

"Get back."

"Liam!"

Turning us around just in time, I see *him* sucker-punching Max in the face. He stumbles back, his hands reaching for his nose.

*Oh. My. God.*

"I'll give you that one," Max says, straightening on his feet when he's barely able to dodge the second blow that swings his way.

A minute ago, *he* was still in control.

But, now, he's lost it completely.

Absolutely lethal.

Only when he tackles Max to the ground do Matthew and Dean decide to interfere.

As if they were completely okay with *him* hitting Max ten seconds ago.

As if they wanted to hit him just as much.

"And don't you ever come near her again," *he* hisses as Matthew and Dean pull *him* off and away from Max, who remains on the ground. "I'm fine," *he* assures them as they let go. "Just fine," he repeats, eyes locked on me.

That's when I realize that Max was his first victim.

And I'm next.

# Chapter 42
## LIAM

How Matthew can calmly sit behind the wheel when we're in the middle of a shitstorm is beyond my comprehension.

But I envy how he's kept it together. I'm usually the one everyone can rely on, the one who knows what to say, how to act, eyes on the goal.

Yet when it comes to people who dominate my mind, who've crawled into my soul, who've stolen a piece of my heart, I lose the reins.

Mix it with a lack of sleep, a minimum of food, and you have me, an impulsive guy who would fuck it all up.

Too impatient to see the bigger picture.

Too restless to wait until the right moment.

Too lost to see a way out.

Because I love her.

Watching her in the rearview mirror, I realize my sanity is sitting right there.

Safe and sound.

I just have to make her see that she can't hide.

Not from me.

# Chapter 43
## LAUREN

We've arrived at the new location—a small, abandoned highway restaurant that looks a lot better on the inside than it does on the outside.

The softly padded retro-look leather booths on the right side, the bar and chrome barstools on the left, the few tables in between—they all seem brand-new.

"Take a seat," Matthew says as he motions to the first booth lined up against the wall.

As much as I want to participate in this conversation, I want Kate to be comfortable. Seeing her slide into the booth, I follow right behind, grabbing ahold of her hand while everyone piles into the diner, and two sides are formed.

Levi, Max, Mr. Rabbit, and one other man—who is apparently Team Vance's driver—line up against the bar while Matthew, Mason, *him*, Jaden, and Colin form a wall in front of our booth. Only Dean isn't here, he's keeping guard outside.

Team Vance and Team SPISe are in a standoff, and nobody is tempted to sit down.

"We're here to help," Matthew starts off.

"We're doing fine on our own," Mr. Rabbit retorts, the very crowded diner filling up with male tension.

"Ten minutes," Matthew says calmly. "And keep an open mind. Think about their safety instead of Vance's orders."

Mr. Rabbit doesn't say a word, he only nods once.

"Lauren and Kate can't stay together," he starts off.

Still sitting in the booth next to my sister, I make an attempt to jump up, but Kate pulls me back down.

Yet I can't stop the words that fly out of my mouth. "No. Way."

Completely disregarded by Team SPISe who still have their backs to me, Matthew continues, "Frank Calvetti is still out there. He wants to kill Vance's children, but he's convinced he's already killed one of them. We have to use that to our advantage. We have to stop him from finding out Kate's alive. And the best way to do that is to keep them separated."

Even though the temperature in the room is rising with each passing second, I get chills all over my body at the name of the man who's done so much damage to our lives, who's still out there, determined to fulfill his promise. Yet the fact that I could be endangering my sister by staying with her is what keeps echoing in my mind.

Only a second ago, I had one outcome in mind—Kate and me together. But, now, I agree with Matthew. Even though we've only had four measly days and I want so much more, I have to let her go.

"Frank is surely monitoring Vance. He's not the ideal person to keep them safe. That's why I've asked a friend to hide Kate. Lauren can stay with us since she's already settled in."

*Now, that's something I will object to.*

Even though no one is facing me, I speak up, "For Kate, I agree. For me, not so much. Just find another great friend who can give me a place to stay."

Matthew turns around, finally regarding me. Even though he remains calm, it doesn't go unnoticed that I've hit a nerve. And he's not the only one who's bristling at my words. Mason's arm is the barrier that stops *him* from marching over.

"I've told you before, and I'll tell you again, family comes first, and after everything we've been through, Lauren, *you are family*," Matthew, the negotiator, says.

My sister remains quiet by my side, her hand squeezing mine, while I fight off Matthew's words with what I've learned just days ago.

"You don't get paid to take care of family," I snap.

This isn't the time or place to bring it up. Yet I'm so heated that I've lost control, focused on getting my way regardless of the means.

"You're right," he says, unwavering. "That's why we refused payment the moment you came to live with us."

"Vance told me—"

"Vance will do and say everything he can to keep you close. I can guarantee you that we haven't accepted a penny since you moved in."

A mixture of relief and disappointment swirls inside my stomach.

Somehow, I want to doubt his words, a reason to stay away from them, from *him,* but I can't. Every bone in my body believes Matthew is telling the truth, scaring me in a way that encourages me to repeat myself, "I want someone else."

"Lauren," Kate whispers.

"I remember telling you something else that day, making you a promise—" Matthew doesn't finish his sentence as I've started shaking my head, trying to stop him from saying it out loud, remembering every single word of his promise.

*"If you so much as take a step out of this building, if that's even possible, I'll find you and bring you back."*

"I'm here to keep that promise."

Breathing is such a simple, unconscious act, but now, it feels as if I have to command each and every one I take.

Matthew regards me a second longer before he turns back around. "So, tell me, convince me that what you're doing is smart, that doing all of this is the best option for them," Matthew says, leaving me off the hook, which means the subject is closed.

A done deal.

"I'm not the one who makes the final decisions," Mr. Rabbit answers.

"You made one just now, moving to this location. At least you have your own opinion."

"I get what you're saying, but—"

"How do we get in touch with Vance?"

"I'll call him," Max answers instead. Phone in hand, he doesn't wait for Mr. Rabbit's permission as he pushes through the swinging doors, heading for the kitchen.

Matthew grabs his cell as well.

"We're done," he says to the person on the other end of the line before he ends the call.

Only a minute later, a couple enters the diner.

"What the hell?" Mr. Rabbit yells, drawing his gun.

"It's okay. They're with me," Matthew assures, as everyone on Team Vance is armed by now.

"You could've given them a heads-up." A well-built, dark-haired man smiles as he saunters toward us, a tall woman with curly red hair walking by his side.

"Lauren, Kate, this is Sam and his wife, Helen," Matthew explains, introducing the couple to us.

Helen slips into our booth on the opposite side of us.

"Kate, you can stay with them until everything's resolved."

Helen holds out a hand toward Kate, getting acquainted with her, as I remain silent, slightly comforted that she'll stay with a couple because I know Kate wants to be part of a family. A home to go to. All things that I have.

Kate would love Sarah. She would embrace the love of all of them.

It makes no sense.

Completely unfair that I get something she wants.

But it's not negotiable.

Matthew has made that crystal clear while *he* doesn't need to say a word.

Even though he's kept his distance—with a *little* help from Mason—I've noticed the dark glances. He would never let me switch places with Kate.

"It will take Vance one hour—two hours, tops—to get here," Max explains as he walks back into the room.

"Great. We'll be gone by then," Matthew answers.

"What?" Mr. Rabbit snaps. "You're not leaving without his permission."

"Waiting for Vance to arrive, knowing he can be trailed, is even more dangerous," Matthew points out.

This was never debatable.

Matthew never intended on waiting for Vance's permission. They came to get me and Kate with or without Vance's consent.

"You can't do this. Vance will never agree," Mr. Rabbit goes on.

"And yet, we will. Lauren is family. And Vance isn't thinking straight. He'll thank me later for making the right decision."

My eyes slide to every guy on SPISe's side. With Helen and Sam, Max and his friends are very much outnumbered. They could never stop them.

"Lauren, it's time to go," Matthew says in a soft yet resolved voice.

As bad as I want to refuse this whole arrangement, I know I have no choice, as every second lingering here could be dangerous for all of us.

Pushing up from the bench, I make one last demand. "Can I have a moment alone with Kate?"

Matthew's frown across his forehead increases. "You can have a moment with Kate," he repeats.

Leaving out one specific word.

The one based on trust.

"I'll stay," Mason says.

"No," *he* objects, moving toward me. "I'll stay."

Diverting my gaze, I reach out to my sister and pull her into my arms while everyone piles out of the diner. I'm determined to spend every second with her in my arms. Only Kate thinks differently, breaking off our hug that could've lasted a lot longer. She steps back, away from me and toward the guy I've been trying to avoid all night.

"I owe you a thank-you," she says out of the blue, standing in front of him. "You saved my life."

Frozen in place, I can only watch, take notice of how he's semi-leaning against the table behind him, his hands squeezing the edge of the table, eyes set on Kate who wraps her arms around him.

She starts off with a rather gentle hug, as if she's afraid he'll push her away.

Instead, he wraps his arms around her, engulfing her with his body.

That's when it happens—when I lose vision of what I see before my eyes.

When the face of my sister starts to fade.

And I only see *him* with a woman in his arms.

How every fiber of my body urges me to jump in.

While my mind is trying to convince me that they're made for each other.

A girl who would never deny his help.

Who would never fight his every move.

A perfect couple.

The thought alone urges me to run.

I'm about to do just that when Kate lowers her arms, taking a small step back, fiddling with her hands, as if she's still coming down from their hug.

"So, you're the guy Lauren's in love with," she says as she stares up at him.

Not a question, but a declaration.

I'm slowly shaking my head, dumbfounded.

"I know I have no right to ask for more when you've given so much already. But, I hope, and think, my favor won't be that much of a burden to you," she goes on as I tighten my hands into fists.

"But she's done so much for me in the past. My big sister, always there for me," she continues while I fight back the tears burning hot in my eyes. "She's always taken care of me, disregarding her own needs. It's time someone looks out for her," she says to him with a voice so strong and confident. "Please, take good care of her," she begs as a lone tear trails down my cheek.

"Although I should warn you." She chuckles through her own tears. "She's stubborn as hell. She'll fight you with everything she has." She sniffs. "But know that, the more she fights back, the closer you're getting."

*He* hasn't said a word, too busy listening to Kate, taking it all in.

Now, his eyes find me.

A Lauren without a wall around her, as Kate just tore it down.

A vulnerable, naked version of myself set in a bright spotlight, as I can't feel anything but uncomfortable. Breakable.

Setting her eyes on me, Kate sobs, "I'm sorry, sis, but you've done so much for me. You've made so many sacrifices. It's time I did something for you. It's time *he* does this for you."

As much as I hate the words she's saying, what she's asking of him, I can *never* hate her.

Kate walks toward me before she pulls me in for a hug and says, "Everything is going to be fine."

Something I've said about a million times.

But now, she's the one saying it to me.

Comforting me.

My renewed sister, how she's stronger, how she's changed.

And I'm sure the universe has altered.

And we've switched places.

# CHAPTER 44
## LIAM

I saw red from the moment she ran away from us.

My mind was set on one thing.

I'd get her back, and I would do it my way.

Once we had the address, I couldn't be reasoned with.

Scaring the shit out of them with our little explosion lessened the tension that'd been ripping my body apart.

It was madness, uncalled for, but the whole team had supported my plan. Solid proof that Kate and Lauren weren't safe with them.

But, most of all, I wanted to send Lauren a message.

Frighten her to the point where she was incapable of putting herself in harm's way. Ever again.

Now, we're inside the car, bathed in darkness with only the streetlights giving me enough clarity to see how she lays her head onto my shoulder, her eyes closed.

As much as I want to give her my anger I had stashed away, I can't stop myself from wrapping my arm around her shoulder, squeezing her body close to mine.

Savoring this moment of peace.

To not only see, but also feel that she's here.

Safe.

For now, I'll hold her and fucking pray that Kate's right.

*"The more she fights back, the closer you're getting."*

If so, then I'm doing all right.

I just have to convince the runner inside of her.
That the right direction is toward me.
And not away.

# Chapter 45
## LAUREN

Hearing my sister bare her heart, saying good-bye, the events of this whole night—it's a lot to take in.

There's no energy left in me to fight *him* and Mason, as they put me in the middle of them on the backseat.

No strength left to fight this all-consuming sleep, my head lolling forward every time until it finally settles on something at my left side, which is just about the right height, the perfect spot.

Feeling a brush along my neck, the warmth of a hand on my right arm, a soothing warmth engulfs me.

And I fall into a blissful sleep.

In the arms of a guy who knows my name.

Feels my pain.

And I don't even bother to care.

# CHAPTER 46
## LAUREN

"What the hell were you thinking?"

About an hour ago, I managed to slip out of bed without waking Liam.

Breathing slowly, eyes closed, lips slightly apart, he was still fast asleep while I was wide awake, dreading our first talk.

All too restless to remain in bed and risk disturbing his much-needed sleep, I tiptoed out the door.

When I look at him now, standing at the end of the long, glossy white dining table, shirtless with only black boxers hugging his thighs, it's as if he immediately jumped out of bed and ran here the moment he opened his eyes.

*He thought I'd run again.*

As the anger swiftly clouds the fear in his eyes, I brace myself for the oncoming lecture. Yet I'd rather not do it with Mason sitting across from me and Liam barely clothed.

"Maybe you should get dressed first," I suggest politely.

"Maybe you should tell me why you left," he fires back.

As if my brain is taking a nap, I ask, "Our bed or this building?"

*Did I just use our?*

"Me."

Shaking my head, I brush away the first wave of guilt.

"Maybe I should leave you two to it," Mason says, unsure as he rises from his chair.

I've changed my mind. With Liam as intimidating as he is right now, I want Mason to stay.

"No," I plead as Liam snaps, "Yes."

Still, Mason takes his plate and walks away.

*Traitor.*

Slamming both hands on the table, Liam repeats his question, "Why did you do it?"

"I had no choice."

"You did." Every muscle in his arms tenses. "He asked you."

"What?"

"Max told us everything."

"He gave me an option I couldn't refuse," I throw back. "I had to see Kate."

"So, someone corners you in a toilet and shows you a video on his smartphone, and you just follow him?" he fumes, pushing away from the table before he prowls in my direction.

Slowly rising from my chair, I intend on keeping a certain distance between us while having this conversation. "Max isn't just someone—"

"No, he isn't," he seethes. "He's Vance's fucking mole—"

"Who you guys hired," I point out. "Besides, the video seemed legit."

"Seemed legit?" he repeats with a dangerous tone.

Still retreating backward, I stumble over Mason's freaking shoes while Liam gains ground fast. "Kate had Sarah's Post-it note."

"Fuck, Lauren. That video could've been a fake one. You could've been running into the hands of Frank fucking Calvetti," he hisses, closing his eyes before opening them back again with a different intensity. "You could've been across the country by now."

I have tons of replies.

Multiple answers.

Yet there isn't one that would erase the fear embedded into his eyes.

Another wave of regret washes over me, and I do the only thing that is right in this situation, the opposite of what I've been trying to do.

I take a step closer to him. "I'm here."

"You could've been killed," he deadpans, his chest rising and falling in a fast rhythm.

"I wasn't," I soothe him by grabbing ahold of his hand.

He remains unmoving as a thick silence envelops us.

"You can't do this again," he says, yanking me close and squeezing me into a hug.

"I know," I whisper, my cheek on his chest.

"I would've found a way," he tells me. "I would've helped you in getting Kate back."

"I'm sorry."

Leaning in to kiss my forehead, he accepts my apology before he finishes, "Because there's really nothing I wouldn't do for you."

His message slams into my chest.

Sliding in the direction of my heart.

# CHAPTER 47
## MATTHEW

"Matthew, I've got a Vance Newman on the line for you," Sarah says with a strained voice.

Enough of an indication that Mr. Newman is very much outraged, which isn't entirely weird since I've declined his calls until we were back home.

"Put him through."

"Where are they?"

I tear the phone a bit further away from my ear before I answer, "Hello, Vance."

"Answer me."

"We've got Kate in a safe house, and Lauren is staying with us."

"I want them both back."

"Vance, let's be smart about this. Let us help you. That way, you have more time to nail Frank."

He doesn't reply.

"Let's work together. You *need* our help."

"I can handle it."

"You can't catch Frank and take care of your daughters at the same time. It's too dangerous." And I won't let him. "I get it. You're their father, and you want to take care of them, but—"

"Fine," he interrupts me.

*That went fast.*

"But I want Levi back with Kate. And I want Max back with you."

"That's not possible."

Max betrayed us. Even if I did give him a second chance, I know someone who would definitely strangle him the second he set foot in this building.

"Take it or leave it."

Shaking my head, I state the truth, "I can't guarantee Max's safety."

"You tell Ressler to deal with Max, or he'll deal with me instead. Because, if Max isn't there, I'll keep coming until I have her back. Until I have them both back."

"Liam isn't his only enemy here," I state, not fond of the idea of reinstating a guy who betrayed us only a few days ago.

"I'll give you my word. He'll be working for you only. I just expect him to keep me updated."

The fact that he wants Max here is clear proof of his distrust, a mutual feeling.

So, I give him a fair last warning. "If you betray us one more time, I'm completely done working with you. Not with Lauren. She's family now. You should know that Liam won't be the only one who'll fight for her."

A painful silence.

"Agreed."

# Chapter 48
## LAUREN

Placing my five tiles onto the Scrabble board, I say every letter before I look up at Liam to announce the word I just formed, the one I had to pass several rounds for just so I could look him in the eye and say, "Loser."

Sarah, Mason, Liam, and I have been playing Scrabble for over an hour. Even though I wasn't thrilled at the idea, I've been liking it a lot, especially because Liam is in fact a loser. A sore loser. I have had more points than him since I managed to form a word with all the letters on my rack, gaining fifty points at once.

"Stop it, you two," Sarah says, smacking my arm before she places *valiance* onto the board. The true winner of this game, she's got a score that is much higher than anyone else's. Apparently, she's a genius, creating words I didn't even know existed.

It's Mason's turn when Liam's phone starts ringing. Picking it up, he walks off, as he usually does. And I follow right behind, as I usually do.

"Yes," he answers to a question I couldn't hear.

Walking beside him, I ask, "Who is it?"

"Yes, she's here," he says as he walks into our room.

"Is it Kate?"

He pulls his phone from his ear before he hands it out to me. "Keep it short."

Grabbing ahold of his phone, I assure him, "I will."

He softly kisses me on my forehead and reluctantly walks out of the room. He hates leaving me to myself. But, more than that, he resents the fact that he can't hear every word of our conversation. Even though our talks are never a secret, I want to be alone for the simple reason that I can't talk about him when he's sitting right beside me.

"Lauren, are you there?"

Plopping down onto the bed, my back against the headboard, I tap the screen to switch to video call before I wave at my sister. "I'm here."

"Everything okay?" she asks, a little worried.

"Of course."

"Then, why the frown?"

"Liam still doesn't like our phone calls. Afraid that we're plotting some kind of grand scheme."

"As if we could do anything by calling each other." Kate chuckles.

"Exactly." *I'm sure I could find a way, but I would never involve my sister.*

"How are you holding up? Are they treating you right?"

"I'm fine, sis. Sam and Helen are great!" she says with a smile.

Yet I wouldn't be her sister if I didn't notice her high-pitched voice, the one she uses when she's trying to mask her true feelings. Or the fleck of sadness in her eyes, the one that's been growing ever since we started calling each other.

It's been over a month since we parted. The distance between us, moving from Vance's house to living with a couple of strangers—all of it has taken its toll. She's slowly fading into a person who doesn't resemble Kate at all.

She won't admit it, or maybe she's unaware, but I can see the signs, the direction she's heading. I saw it happen after the loss of our mother, and I can't be a bystander again.

"Don't do anything stupid," my sister says, disturbing my thoughts.

"What?"

"You've got that face."

"What face?" *The one that displays that I'm busy looking for a solution?* "It's my I-care-for-my-baby-sister face. Nothing to worry about."

"I know it is," she sighs. "And that's *exactly* why I'm worried. You tend to do a lot of crazy things for your *baby* sister."

I wasn't handed a lot of patience when I was born.

Somehow, Kate ended up with the whole lot while I just got a mind capable of conjuring wicked plans combined with a body that can't seem to sit still when it should.

As result, I've decided that, as of today, I'm done waiting for them to handle Frank.

It's time I take matters into my own hands.

Time to give in to my body and mind.

Time to set my plan in motion.

# Chapter 49
## LAUREN

I'm in the critical OCR. A restricted area. But, since I'm considered family now and because Max isn't allowed here, I've been a regular visitor for the past few months, hanging out in the small lounge area, watching Netflix while Liam is working.

A crucial mistake, giving me access to a place where all the critical information is being dealt with, including the Frank Calvetti case.

Although I haven't found out a single thing this past month, I feel the odds are in my favor today with Liam being called away and Brice—a SPISe operative who takes regular shifts in the control room—in crisis mode.

"Matthew, we've got a problem," Brice says, pulling a grim face, his phone in hand. "Yeah, the server isn't accessible. Or there's a problem with the connection." He pauses. "Or we just lost a ton of files."

Even though I'm not an IT know-it-all, I know enough to realize this is bad, grave enough for Brice to forget about me.

They've been careful around me, locking down their computers when they go to the toilet, halting their conversations when I enter the room.

But, right now, Brice is losing his mind over some server malfunction, forcing him to leave the room, and I have it all to myself for the very first time.

This control room, which is specifically for critical operations, is normally manned by two or three persons on a twenty-four/seven basis. The fact that Brice is alone at the moment and that Liam had to leave is a clear sign that something is going on.

But it's an opportunity for me to retrieve information.

A moment I've been waiting for.

Getting up from the couch, I walk straight to Brice's computer, which hasn't been locked down. The task bar is filled with folders, but only one stands out.

The Frank Calvetti case. I throw another glance at the screen above the door, a live video feed of an empty hallway leading up to the OCR entrance.

*I'm good—for now.*

When I open the folder, the screen fills with about twenty subfolders.

All the information, just one click away. My window of time, unknown.

Clicking on *Frank Calvetti*, the only folder that probably contains what I need, I get another screen filled with files, and I pick the one on top—*Personal Information.*

Scrolling through it, I find a whole lot of text, an address of a company named RS Construction, which is located in San Bernardino, and two phone numbers.

Grabbing a pen and a Post-it note, I write down the phone numbers, not the address. Even if he's linked to it somehow, I can't fly across the state without any money or my ID.

I've just scribbled it down when I notice movement on the video feed. Luckily, Brice still needs a five-digit code and a card to open the door. It's enough time for me to close the file, turn back to the original folder, and minimize it before I skid back to the couch, crumbling up the note as I stuff it into the side pocket of my jeans.

Throwing myself back down onto the couch, I manage to take the same position as before while Brice walks in.

"Yeah, nothing to worry about," says the man who has recovered his smile. "You fixed it?" I ask him once he gets off the phone.

Falling back in his chair, he nods as he notices his *little* error—probably because he didn't have to enter his password.

Eyes slightly narrowed, he casts them in my direction, scrutinizing my position and my facial expression before he slightly shakes his head. He sets his eyes back on his screen, seemingly convinced that I didn't just skim through his files.

Unaware that the smoldering plan inside my mind just received tons of oxygen.

A spark to my already-wicked idea.

I can only hope I won't get burned.

# Chapter 50
## MATTHEW

I'm in my office with Sebastian, going over my newfound information, when Anna—Sarah's substitute since she has the day off—calls in to let me know, "Lauren is here. She wants to talk to you in private."

We see each other out of the office on a regular basis. The fact that Lauren's at my door, demanding a meeting, means it's either urgent or very important.

"Send her in," I say to Anna before I look at Sebastian. "We'll finish this later."

As Sebastian walks out of the office, Lauren walks in, taking her place in one of the two chairs in front of my desk.

"How can I help you, Lauren?"

Instead of answering right away, she gazes outside, another confirmation that something's wrong. But I know Lauren. If I push her too hard, she'll fall back, and then I won't know what's going on in that head of hers.

That's why I respect her silence until she asks the one question I get at least once every week.

"Have you found him yet?"

I get it. It must be hard to deal with all of this, especially when you've been doing whatever you wanted your whole life—until now. She's been forced to rely on us, all the while separated from her sister and unaware that we're not only dealing with Frank Calvetti—a real madman, who presumably murdered his own brother-in-law—but we're also dealing with the Mafia. The man married into it the day he made Rebecca Rossi his wife, which forces us to take on their whole organization to get him. The biggest operation we've done so far. One we can't handle on our own, so both Vance's team and the FBI are on it, too.

"I'm sorry, Lauren, but we haven't."

It's all she needs to know now.

The whole SPISe team agreed that there's no use in explaining to her the complexity of the situation. It wouldn't change a single thing. It'd only make her life more miserable.

"Use me."

Sipping from my already-cold coffee, I almost choke when I hear her say those words. "What?"

Assuming I didn't get the message the first time, she repeats, "You can use me to draw him—"

"Lauren," I say her name with a firm tone while I get up from my chair, stopping her from finishing her sentence, as I'm unable to let her make that ridiculous suggestion twice. "Your life isn't a fiction movie," I say as I walk around my desk toward her, trying to keep my voice as neutral as possible. "There aren't any guaranteed happy endings. Especially when you start considering such options."

"You're right," she admits way too fast as she jumps up from her chair, about to make a run for it.

Placing a hand on the desk, I get in her way. Only one purpose in mind, I have to nip this thought in the bud. One she chose to share with me instead of Liam, as his reaction wouldn't have been as mild as mine.

"It's not the first time I have to remind you of my promise. And it probably won't be the last time either." I pause, seeing she's busy looking at anything but me. "It's time I make you a new promise," I say as I grab ahold of her upper arm, getting her full attention. "We'll find him. I'll make sure of it," I finish, giving her arm a gentle squeeze.

Staring into my eyes, she nods before she says, "Thank you."

Even though I'm not entirely convinced that she will let this go, I let her walk out of my office.

More determined than ever to deal with Frank.

To get all that scum off the street.

Because, if they think we're afraid, they haven't met the SPISe family.

At least, not yet.

# Chapter 51
## LAUREN

Three weeks ago, I walked out of Matthew's office with a plan in mind, a crumpled paper in my pocket, and the realization that I'm on my own.

I just had to suggest it to Matthew, had to give it a shot.

Because I needed SPISe to have my back.

Because I wanted Liam's support, and I thought Matthew could convince him.

Yet he declined.

I've done my best to let this go, tried to battle the wicked voices in my head. But, when they start making sense, giving me another plausible plan, I know I'm lost already.

So, I've made the decision, the one nobody's been able to make.

And I get it. I couldn't do it either if it were someone else's life.

But this is about mine.

My choice to make.

My risk to take.

My life on the line.

And I have only one goal in mind.

*Get the bastard.*

With sweaty hands and a hair bun that is painfully tight, I now see the danger, the loose ends, the endless list of things that could go wrong.

Yet it's too late to back down.

Too late to call it off.

Everything's been set up; almost every step in my plan has been finished.

Gazing at the people around me, I have to deal with the choices I've made.

Live with the fact that I've ruined my first—but hopefully not my last—date with Liam, so I can execute my plan.

# Chapter 52
## LIAM

*Seventeen Hours Earlier*

A first date should be special, especially since it's something Lauren vowed she'd never do, which is a huge step forward in our relationship.

Yet I've been solely focused on the necessary security measures.

I've picked out the least popular movie, a biographical sports film, in one of the smallest indie movie theaters in New York on a Monday night, just so we'll have the whole auditorium to ourselves.

*The fewer people around us, the fewer threats.*

I've been keeping an eye on the entrance the whole time instead of acknowledging my beautiful girlfriend sitting right next to me.

And, although I have one arm wrapped around her shoulders, I keep my right hand on my knee, free to reach out to my gun, if necessary.

All of it, ideal ways to ruin a special first date.

Now that the end credits are rolling over the screen and we're walking toward the exit, I regret every glance away from her.

"Did you like the movie?" I ask as I grab her hand, stopping her from leaving the auditorium, as I'm not ready for our first date to end.

"I did." She nods, looking toward the doors, which swing closed as Matthew and Sarah, the only remaining people, exit the room. Yet another security measure. "Did you actually *see* anything of the movie?" she asks, her hazel eyes connecting with mine.

Apparently, my tension and the many glances toward the exit haven't gone unnoticed. "Lovely movie." I smile, my lie as obvious as the light of day.

My hands on her hips, I steer her toward the dark fabric-paneled wall before her back hits it, and I'm looming over her.

"You sure like me in this position." She grins, although I see a glint of nervousness in her eyes.

"Yes, I do." I close the distance between us. "Because I love to have you as close as possible." I pause. "And because, this way, I'm sure you won't run," I add.

A flash of sadness washes over her face, making me regret my stupid remark.

"I'm such an—"

With the unfinished sentence, she takes my face in her hands before she crushes her lips against mine, pouring all her bottled-up emotions into this one kiss.

Parting my lips, I fiercely kiss her back, her soft moan coursing throughout my whole body.

"Can you two do this at home, please?" Matthew interrupts as he pushes open the door. "We've got to make room for the late-night movie crowd." He smirks before he steps back out.

At least I've made three minutes of our date memorable.

"Let's go home."

Lauren nods reluctantly.

Putting an arm around her shoulders, I tuck her into my side as we exit the cinema.

Wearing a smile as bright as the sun on a scorching hot day.

Because of our first date.

A grand success.

Because of Lauren.

A whole different person.

# Chapter 53
## LAUREN

*Sixteen Hours Earlier*

"Thank you," I blurt out when Liam takes his place behind the wheel, cranking the engine.

"For what?" he asks blankly, eyes following Matthew's car, who is peeling out of the parking lot, before he sets eyes back on me.

"For tonight," I answer. It's such a cliché thing to say, yet it's the truth. As much as I've been using our first real date to set my plan into motion, I haven't faked a thing.

Every word out of my mouth has been straight from the heart.

Every move I've made is genuine.

No discussions, not one argument, as I've been too busy cherishing every minute in his presence, every second of our first date that I'm about to ruin.

A deep frown puckering his forehead, his eyes slightly darker, he asks, "Are you okay?"

The word *no* is on the tip of my tongue, as I'm almost tempted to explain everything and ask him for help. He's the expert after all.

The guy who would move heaven and earth for me.

Except for this.

He would never allow what I'm about to do.

He would never stand on the sidelines while I risked my life.

“Lauren?”

Biting my tongue, I look straight forward. “I’m fine.” My eyes are set on the fro-yo shop, which is about forty-five feet away, across the parking lot.

“What is it?”

Swallowing down the truth, I ask, “Do you mind getting me a frozen yogurt with blueberries?”

He looks at the shop and then back at me. “You want a frozen yogurt with blueberries?”

I nod, eyes still averted.

“Right now?”

I nod again, composing myself before I set my eyes on him.

He scrutinizes my face. “All right.” Liam sighs. “Let’s go get one.”

Cutting the engine, he reaches for his door when I place the flat of my hand against his chest.

“It’s okay. I’ve changed my mind.”

“What?” He shakes his head. “Why? You just said you wanted one.”

*Oh God, this isn’t turning out the way I wanted.*

“I don’t feel like getting out of the car again. My muscles are still sore from running yesterday.” I shrug. “Besides, it won’t do me any good. Too many calories.” Such a woman thing to say, yet I want him to get out of the car without me.

Seeing how he hesitates, I know he’s trying to figure out a way to get me my yogurt without leaving me alone, which is impossible since there aren’t any free parking spaces closer to the shop.

“First of all, you don’t need to lose weight. And second, I’ll go and get you one. Just stay here and if something’s wrong, honk.”

He’s about to get out, exactly what I need him to do, yet I can’t let him go. My hand still resting on his chest, I shift closer, pressing a short kiss to his jawline before I reluctantly pull back.

Even though I want my last kiss to be a memorable one, I can’t push it, afraid that I’ll raise suspicions, if there aren’t any already.

“I’ll get you your yogurt,” he promises.

"Thank you."

*For everything.*

"Be right back," he says, placing one more sweet kiss on my lips before he gets out of the car, locking the doors with the remote.

Walking along the front of the car and onto the pedestrian strip at a rather quick pace, he gives me short glances every ten feet. Even though there are three rows of cars in between us, he still has a view of the car when he reaches the shop.

The whole situation seems harmless when, really, it's not.

I'm about to ruin everything for a needle in a haystack.

Yet I ignore the tears prickling at the backs of my eyes and my heart beating in the back of my throat.

Because this is my chance at getting my sister back, restoring our lives.

A risk I have to take.

Grabbing Liam's spare key out of my purse—the one I found in the bottom drawer of his desk—I'm grateful that Liam agreed to take his Audi instead of the Range Rover, making all of this possible.

Now, I only need to silence my heart to get this show on the road and me away from him.

Shifting my butt over the middle console, I take my place in the driver's seat, putting the key in the ignition as I give him one last glance. He's in the shop, standing in line, eyes on the car but unable to see that I'm behind the wheel and not in the passenger seat. Unable to hear me starting the engine.

Only when I start to reverse the car do I notice the bunched eyebrows, the eyes filled with disbelief, as every beautiful moment we just shared splatters to the ground.

But the thing that tears me apart is knowing that, while I've been relentless about rebuilding a wall, he's never had one.

With his vow to not back down any longer came a free pass to his heart.

One I'm about to destroy by leaving him again.

*Forgive me.*

I've rarely done something in my life I so much resented.

But pulling out of the parking spot while Liam is sprinting toward me, covering the distance extremely fast as I'm pushing the pedal to the metal, is the hardest thing I've ever done.

Yet it's the slap of his hand against the rear window of the car as I peel away that shatters my fragile heart.

The only thing I didn't even know I had.

Tears trailing down my cheeks, I stomp on the gas to get off the lot and onto the street as I take one more glance in the rearview mirror, displaying a livid Liam, who's at a complete standstill in the middle of the parking lot with a cell phone to his ear.

*And so it begins.*

From now on, every second is crucial, and every move has to be calculated. I'm still wearing my bracelet with a tracker in it, as Liam gave it back after our talk. And even though Liam's car isn't a company car, I'm not entirely sure that this car hasn't got a device, too.

Weaving in and out of traffic, I wipe away my tears and hope it'll take Matthew at least ten minutes to pick up Liam. Because that's the amount of time I give myself to wash away this horrible feeling, ditch this car, and lose my trackers.

I've learned from the best after all.


It's been two hours since I left Liam. Enough confirmation that I'm not wearing any other trackers. And I've made good progress, running a steady pace, getting a good distance away from where I left the car.

I even went into a Walmart where I bought a pair of sunglasses, a pink baseball cap, ripped jeans, a yellow sweater, and a cheap cell phone with the money I found in my old wallet, which was inside a box with all my other personal stuff.

Plus, I met Jude—a friendly nurse who just ended her night shift—who didn't mind giving me a place to sleep for the night. No questions asked. Saving me from sleeping outside, which wasn't such a good idea to begin with.

As I sit on her couch, my new phone in hand, my finger hovers over the Send button.

*Tomorrow, around four in the afternoon, Vance's daughter Lauren will be shopping at the Westfield Shopping Mall in New York.*

A simple text with an added address, which I send to the two phone numbers I've got—to who I presume is Frank Calvetti.

I hope he'll be so reckless, so blinded by hatred, that he would do quite anything to get his hands on me, including following a lead based on a random text from an unknown number.

Pressing Send, I switch off the phone and lie down on the small couch.

And I realize I've just sentenced myself to death.

If I don't get killed by Frank, Liam will do the job for him.

Covering myself with a small, thin blanket, I can only hope it's the second option.

# CHAPTER 54
## MATTHEW

*Eight Hours Earlier*

With Lauren gone and Liam combing every street in New York City, I was left behind, stuck with a puzzle I couldn't seem to figure out.

There was no camera footage to use, no trackers to follow, leaving us behind with a big, *Why?*

Until ten minutes ago, when I received a text, when everything became crystal clear, and my heart skipped a beat. Or five.

*Be at the Westfield Shopping Mall at 4 p.m. and bring as many men as possible. I've arranged a meet with Frank. Don't kill me. Catch him. I'll text you with more information soon.*

And then another text came seven seconds later.

*I'm sorry.*

*She wouldn't,* my rational mind said.

*She definitely would,* my knowing mind countered, as I still remember her suggesting it in my office.

Even though it's from an unknown number, I have no doubt it's her.

The puzzle pieces fit perfectly, and the big picture is horrifying.

Locking down my anger, I use it to do what I do best—set up a mission while I scrape together every ounce of courage to find Liam and get him on board.

A risk with the way he's acting.

But I know I won't live to see another day if he doesn't get the chance to make this right.
To get her back.
He loves her.
We all do.

# CHAPTER 55
## LAUREN



*Present*

*Choose a meeting place. Check.*

I've picked out the Westfield Shopping Mall. Crowded enough for me to blend in, enough space for the SPISe team to roam around.

*Set up a meeting with Frank. Check.*

I've sent a text. Yet I never got one back, no confirmation that someone's coming. I can only hope.

*Inform Matthew about my insane plan, so they can back me up and catch the bastard. Check.*

I've already seen Jaden and Mason walking around.

Thank God it's a busy Saturday with enough people around for me to blend in. I'm sharing a bench with a mom and her daughter while I'm wearing my new clothes, sunglasses, and a pink cap—it had to be a cap, a reminder of Liam, who used to wear one to disguise himself from me—covering my hair that I've knotted into a low bun. And, since they walked right past me, I've done a good job at disguising myself.

Sitting on a bench in the main hall, I go over my almost-completed checklist in my head as I try to keep my breathing under control and my hands from quivering too much.

I know what I need to do. And, even though I feel sick to my stomach, I'll finish it, knowing that SPISe has my back.

Taking out my cell phone, I boot it up and send one more text.

*Lauren's at the fountain in the main hall.*

I send my exact location to both parties to draw in Frank while I give Matthew's team the exact location where they'll have to be.

As the final straw, the final push to make sure Frank shows up, I take off my pink cap and sunglasses, release my hair from its bun, and rise on shaky legs as I realize how foolishly dangerous this entire mission really is.

My eyes set on the fountain ahead of me, I drag my feet there and notice every person around me.

I'm not only endangering my own life; I'm also involving every other living and breathing human in this shopping mall, including Matthew, Mason, SPISe operatives, and Liam. If Matthew told him.

If only I'd seen the light earlier.

If only I'd had the patience to sit this one out.

But it's too late for what-ifs.

Too late to back down.

My head up high, I have to give it my all while I try to minimize the risks.

I'll be damned if I let anyone get harmed because of me.

I've almost reached the fountain when my cell phone starts ringing.

I haven't been sloppy with remembering to turn it off after texting, a precaution to keep them from tracing me. Yet, now that I've sent both parties my location, it doesn't matter anymore.

With a shaky hand, I put the phone to my ear, ready to make a deal with the devil.

"Lauren."

My heart's doing a marathon inside my chest, but I can't hold back a smile as I hear Matthew's hushed voice.

"Walk away." He sounds out of breath.

*What?*

"Lauren"—he gasps—"leave!"

"Is Frank here? Did you find him?"

There's no answer, and I only have to take four more steps.

Before I'll be a sitting duck.

Before I put my life in someone else's hands.

"Matthew?"

I can hear him talking to someone else while I have just one more step to take.

But I never reach it.

Two arms encircle my waist, lifting me clean off my feet.

Adrenaline floods my veins, and I'm ready to fight back when the stranger speaks up.

"I've got her." Mason's voice rings in my ear.

"Mason," I sigh his name in relief.

He turns me around, setting me on the ground, and then he force-walks me in the direction of the exit, aborting my whole mission, unless they've already finished it.

I stumble along, trying to soothe my erratic heart, as I squeeze his arm. "Did you catch him?"

There's no confirmation as we cover more ground, away from my setup.

Based on the tension of his body, I can only guess they didn't.

"Just give me a little more time. Maybe he'll come," I plead as I turn my head, wanting to look directly into his eyes, which is kind of hard with the way he's holding me.

"No. Fucking. Way. Will you stay here another second," he barks, his voice a deadly hiss.

*No. No. No.*

I freeze. But Mason wants none of that. He solves it by semi-carrying me further away from the fountain.

That's when I realize that Matthew's team isn't here to back me up. They came here to get me out. All my efforts were done in vain, and I'm being dragged through a crowded hallway. People are openly staring or deliberately looking away when only one person stands out.

Perhaps it's because he's running toward me with so much determination. Or maybe it's because it's Liam, and he'll always stand out to me.

Seeing how his eyes zero in on me, how anger is radiating off of him, the guilt I've harbored threatens to spill right out.

When he's almost within arm's reach, I plead for him to look at me, give me a chance to say the words I've repeated a million times in my head these past seventeen hours.

But he never acknowledges me.

Only his cold and distant voice says, "Put this on," as he holds out a leather vest.

I don't have the time to agree, as he's already hanging it around my shoulders, waiting for me to slide my arms through the sleeves before he closes the zipper.

The heaviness of the jacket reminds me of the bulletproof vest I wore when I was with Max, only this one seems to be regular clothing.

"I'll take her," Liam says to Mason, disregarding me.

And so I'm treated as a package.

A delivery from one to the other.

My punishment for ditching him again.

Even though I deserve it, I'd beg for a murderous glance, a fuming lecture, a series of curse words.

Instead, he pulls me along with a roughness that confirms my biggest fear.

I've lost him.

Gone before I ever realized I had him in the first place.

So busy denying what was right in front of me, too fixated on my mother's mistakes, I refused the only person who fought for me.

I stumble along as we exit the mall with Liam by my side and Mason jogging in front of us, heading for the black Ford SUV, for Bryan and Jaden, who are waiting alongside.

My limbs grow heavier with every step I move forward.

Every inch we cover is proof that my whole plan to nail Frank, get back my freedom, be reunited with my sister, and beg for Liam's forgiveness has been ripped to pieces.

One epic fail.

If I go back and give this mission another try, I still have a chance at getting back together with my sister.

Someone to go home to.

Someone who won't treat me as cargo.

So, I halt in the middle of the shopping mall's front lawn, Liam stumbling into me because of my sudden move.

His arm across my stomach and over my chest, he manages to keep us both on our feet as he barks, "Move," into my ear.

Turning around in his arms, I slowly shake my head, digging my nails into his arms. "I want to finish this."

"No way in hell are you going back. Now, move!" he hisses, very much determined as he tries to throw me over his shoulder. A move I barely manage to avoid.

"Let me go."

His eyes are narrowed to thin slits while his arms enclose me, his hands digging firmly into my hips.

He's about to overpower me when something whizzes past me.

"GET DOWN!" Mason screams.

It takes my brain too many seconds to translate two simple words into action.

*Thank God Liam's brain is way faster.*

The moment I realize somebody is in fact shooting at us, I'm already engulfed by him, his right arm squeezing the life out of me while his left arm tucks my face against his chest before he tackles us to the ground.

My heart hammering in my chest, I feel his racing breath along my neck, his whole body pinning me down.

More shots are fired, and people are screaming, but we remain in place. Pandemonium is all around us as I shut my eyes, and hold my breath, my body as still as possible, afraid that I'll screw it up even more.

"We're clear!" Mason yells nearby. "Let's move."

Opening my eyes, I see how Mason is pulling Liam off me while Jaden and Max—who I hadn't noticed before—are hovering above us, guns in hands, eyes set on our surroundings.

A second later, I'm off the ground, in between Liam and Mason as we run over the practically deserted lawn and toward the car with Max and Jaden covering us.

I'm the first one who's shoved into the safe confines of the spacious SUV, followed by Liam and Mason.

Another two seconds, and Max slaps the rear window of the car. We pull away from the curb with Bryan behind the wheel and Jaden in the passenger seat.

Squeezed in between Liam's body and the side of the car, I look into Liam's dark eyes, when the seriousness of this whole situation starts to seep in.

"Are you hurt?" he demands, wincing a little when he starts skimming every inch of my leather vest.

Dread coils in my stomach in a way that feels all too familiar while I see how Mason is trying to get Liam's attention.

"Answer me," he powers through, ignoring Mason's pleas, as if getting my answer is the last thing he'll do.

I slowly shake my head while he zips open my jacket, his hands roaming my entire shirt. Since he has to shift a little closer, I notice the darkened spot on his left upper arm. The smell, still engraved in my memory from the night my sister got shot, confirms that I'm about to relive my worst nightmare.

"You're hit," I whimper, my hand reaching out to touch the bleeding spot on his arm, the one Mason is trying to get ahold of.

But Liam's too busy trying to pull my arms out of my vest as pain flickers across his face.

*No. No. No.*

"Liam!" Mason yells. "Give me your arm!"

*I can't lose him.*

I let him pull my vest off me before I grab ahold of his prying hands.

"I'm fine."

I don't know how much of a statement I can make with shaky hands and tears pooling in my eyes. I can only hope my unwavering voice gets the message across, so he'll stop fussing over me and let Mason take care of him.

He gives me another once-over before his hands slide out of mine. He takes off his own bulletproof jacket, wincing with every move he makes.

"Is it just your arm?" Mason asks, his bloodied hands now applying pressure to the bare wound with Liam's short sleeve rolled up.

"I got hit in the back. My vest stopped it," he explains.

Two bullets meant for me.

But he took them.

He got hurt because of me.

"Here, use this." Jaden gives Mason a belt, so that he can strap it around the wound and close it up. Something to stop his blood from seeping out, to keep him from becoming paler than he already is.

I try to ignore all the signs, be as calm as everyone in this car is, yet still, my heart is pounding a heavy drum, adrenaline drenching my system while a cloak of fear engulfs me.

"Lauren?" Mason's eyes zero in on me.

My lips remain motionless, my eyes fixed on the person who should be overbearing and pissed as hell right now. Instead, he's slumped against the seat, eyes closed, as he takes deep breaths.

"Liam, scoot over," Mason urges, wanting to switch positions, so he can help me get through this panic attack.

"No. No," I plead, drawing in fast, shallow breaths.

"Are you hurt?" Mason asks, still in his current place.

Liam opens his eyes and sets them on me, grabbing my hand and squeezing it. Almost as if he's saying good-bye.

My ears start to buzz; my vision's breeding black spots. But Liam wouldn't be Liam if he didn't notice.

"Lauren, breathe."

He starts to move around, trying to get himself in the same position he always uses when I have a panic attack. He already knows I need the closeness of his body to calm me down.

Since every move seems to hurt him, I vigorously shake my head. "Let me hold you."

That's how he ends up with his head in my lap, his dark eyes beaming into mine. A terrible déjà vu is the trigger for the words I need to say.

"I'm sorry." Tears streaming down my face, I repeat them over and over again. "I'm so sorry."

*For all the fights.*

*For all the lies.*

*For keeping you out.*

*For deceiving you.*

*For running away.*
*For letting you get hurt.*

"This is all my fault." I lean down, my forehead touching his.

Something I've only done with my sister.

But, now, it feels like the right thing to do.

My shoulders shake with every sob while he starts drawing circles on the back of my hand.

I almost choke on the words that come out of my mouth. "I can't lose you."

"Lauren," he whispers, squeezing my hand hard.

With my name on his lips, maybe for the very last time, I finally see what I've hidden inside and how he deserves to see it, too.

How I owe him all of me.

No more lies.

No more barrier.

"I can't lose you," I repeat, pulling my head back because I owe it to him to look him in the eye for what I'm about to say, the words I've vowed never to tell anyone.

But, now, the need to say them is almost tearing me apart.

"I can't lose you." I gasp, scraping all the leftovers of my bravery together.

I'm about to give him my heart and my soul.

I'm about to give him my all.

"I love you."

With the painful squeeze of his hand, the glint of a tear in the corner of his eye, he lifts his head, determined to put his lips on mine.

Drawing my face a bit further out of reach, there's only one more thing I need to say.

"William Drew Ressler," I sob, a new load of tears making their way down, "please don't leave me!"

Instead of answering, he lets go of my hand.

Sliding his hand into my hair, he insistently pushes my mouth to his, my lips instantly parting with the need to kiss him back.

Although we've gone way beyond kissing in the past, I get a taste of the new us.

That is, until we're reminded of our audience.

"You can't get rid of me, Lauren Miller." He grins—the stubborn ass—almost capable of hiding all his pain. "But you're in so much trouble when we get home," he adds, all goofiness gone.

A promise.

One that once would've encouraged me to turn around and run.

But, now, I grab ahold of his hand.

Ready to stay and fight for whatever he's got in store for me.

Ready to fight for us.

# Chapter 56
## LAUREN

If someone had told me a month ago that I'd be fighting with a nurse because I had to leave Liam's side, I would've never believed it.

Yet, today, that's exactly what I'm doing.

"Miss, you have to stay here," she snips at me. Her message is still polite, but the look on her face, not so much.

"I'm sorry, Nurse"—Mason takes a good look at her name tag—"Rosaline, but Lauren and Liam, they're inseparable. You know, first love and all," he finishes, placing an arm around my shoulders as he uses his most charming smile to lessen the tension.

Snapping my mouth closed, I look up at him, glaring.

"Of course. I understand," she chimes, using a whole other tone toward Mason, aka Prince Charming. "I'll let you know as soon as I have an update," she says, walking off.

"You're good at this," I huff, semi-happy that she might be a bit more flexible because of Mason's blue eyes.

"Yes, I am," he says, tugging me a bit closer. "In fact, I'm an expert by now. Eight months ago, I was doing the very same thing for a buddy of mine. You see, his girlfriend crashed her car. She was rushed to the hospital, unconscious, and he didn't know how badly she was hurt. You can imagine how hard it was for him to leave her once we came into the ER." He sighs, coming to a halt.

My car crash.

We never really talked about it; the news of my sister's death made my accident irrelevant.

Now, I'm almost reliving that moment from his point of view.

Experiencing the same fear of losing someone.

And I understand.

"He must've been very angry."

"Angry?" He smirks, steering me toward Bryan and Jaden—who are lingering in the waiting room—his arm still around me. "More like extremely pissed. Started throwing chairs around."

I can imagine him doing exactly that, losing control because of my actions.

"I know you've been through a lot in the past. I know you've fought a lot of battles on your own, taking great care of Kate and yourself. But some battles aren't meant to be fought alone." His arm still wrapped around me, he squeezes my shoulders. "And some battles shouldn't even be considered doing on your own," he says, seriousness covering every single word.

"I know," I agree as we come to a standstill in front of Bryan and Jaden.

"In fact, we're all a bit mad right now," he admits as they all look down on me.

"You can leave out the *bit* part," Jaden adds, ticked off.

Cowering beneath their worried gazes, I'm barely holding it together when Matthew enters the semi-crowded waiting room.

"Let's go," he says. "We're moving to a separate room."

With Matthew leading the way, Mason and I follow him down the hallway where he motions for us to enter a small examination room.

"Bryan and Jaden, wait here. Keep us updated about Liam," Matthew says before he comes inside and closes the door, eyes set on me. "We need to talk."

*I was afraid he'd say exactly that.*

With Mason leaning against the wall, I no longer have his physical or mental support. Yet I refuse to sit down, make myself even smaller than I already am in comparison to them. Instead, I take position in front of the examination table, my hands grabbing ahold of the metal frame behind my back as I remain standing on shaky legs.

"Lauren," he starts off.

My hands tightening around the frame, I brace for the inevitable lecture.

Every passing second he remains quiet is absolutely excruciating.

"I owe you an apology," Matthew says.

Words that should've come out of my mouth.

"I made a mistake," he continues. "I thought that it was better to keep you out of the loop about Frank, that you'd only stress more if you knew all of it." He pauses. "You wouldn't have done what you did today if we'd told you *everything.*" He emphasizes his last word as he sets his worried eyes on me. "The fact is, we know exactly where Frank Calvetti is."

"What?" Shaking my head, I try to tune down the judgment in my voice, remembering the address of a construction firm I saw, yet I thought it was only a hunch. Not a certainty.

"We know where he lives," he says. "We just don't have any proof that he tried to kill Kate. Or you."

"He shot Liam today," I hiss.

"He didn't," he answers immediately.

"What?"

"Frank wasn't at the mall today. Daniel Cameron was. He shot Liam."

Pushing away from the bed, I yell, "Who's Daniel Cameron?"

"Presumably one of Frank's accomplices." He sighs. "You see, Frank Calvetti is married to Rebecca Rossi. Basically, he's married into a powerful Mafia family, running their illegal business through their construction firm. As of today, there are still tons of court cases running against them. They've never been convicted. Too many threats. Witnesses tend to disappear."

*The Mafia?*

"When your father shot Enrico Powell, he not only started a vendetta with Frank, but also with the Mafia." He sighs.

"Frank's got a lot of resources to get what he wants. All that's happened are his orders, but not his doing. The man doesn't do anything himself. And, even if he did, he'd find a way to make it happen without any trail."

Barely blinking, I try to wrap my mind around his words while my teeth dig into my lip until I taste the copper inside my mouth.

"We've thought about framing him for something, but even if we get him behind bars, there will be someone else to continue his work."

Pushing away from the bed, I cry out in exasperation, "So, we do nothing?"

"We are doing everything we can to catch them all, which is extremely complicated and risky."

My whole mission to lure Frank out, to get him behind bars was ridiculous.

Suicide.

Because of my irrational actions, I endangered them all.

Because of my foolishness, Liam got hurt.

"Lauren," Mason pleads, all of a sudden in front of me, his hands on my shoulders, "breathe."

Guilt drowns me in giant waves.

"I'll go get a nurse," Matthew speaks up, and I hear the sound of a door opening.

"No!" I gasp, grabbing on to Mason's arms while I seek Matthew out. "I'll be fine," I assure him, although my fingers dig deeper into Mason's skin.

Matthew is about to disregard my announcement when I speak up again, "I'm sorry." Tears pop up in the corners of my eyes.

Shifting my eyes to Mason, I want them both to know, "I'm sorry."

Mason's blue eyes are calm and soothing, full of forgiveness. "I know, sis," he answers. "I know," he repeats once more as his thumb brushes away a fallen tear. The first of many, as I can't contain them any longer.

Too many times, I've fought them.

Countless occasions, I've denied them.

Now, as Mason pulls my head against his chest, they run freely.

"Don't worry; we'll get the bastard. He'll pay for what he's done. You just need to let us handle it. Let us take care of you. And Kate."

My arms curling around him, I embrace him, never thinking I would ever have more than one sibling, a family.

One who cares so much that they would forfeit their own lives to save mine.

# CHAPTER 57
## LIAM

Sharing a small hospital bed with Lauren isn't very comfortable.

Yet I wouldn't want it any different than to feel her body pressed against mine as I see the rise and fall of her chest with every breath she takes.

Because the fact is, I could be missing a leg, and I'd still feel complete with her in my arms—or arm since my left arm is in a sling.

From the moment Lauren drove off during our date to Matthew telling me what she was up to while unable to stop her, I've never felt so helpless, furious, and afraid at once.

As a zombie, I drove around New York, looking for her.

As a robot, I executed every step of Matthew's plan once we knew where she would be.

As a professional, I herded her to the getaway car, disregarding the bullet penetrating my arm or the one that hit my vest.

I only had one priority.

Get *her* to safety as soon as possible.

The girl who made running away from me her new hobby.

Who cost me ten years of my life for all the things she'd done.

Who held me in her arms, terrorized by the same fear I'd had one too many times.

Who waited until I got shot to open up to me, to give me the words I'd been dying to hear.

*"I love you."*

Words that breathed life back into my body.

A message that reanimated my heart and made me open my eyes.

She was alive.

Unharmed.

Safe.

All the tension and anger left my body, and I was finally able to feel again, embracing the moment regardless of the difficulties we'd had.

That is, until we walked into the ER, and I was carted off, forced to say good-bye again, anxious at the thought of leaving her out of my sight.

"I'm not taking my eyes off her," Mason assured me with a determined look. One he'd had ever since she ran away. "We will all be watching her." He motioned to Bryan and Jaden as he squeezed my right shoulder before walking in Lauren's direction, who was having a heated talk with the head nurse.

It was her first but definitely not her last, since she fought with every single nurse who complained about her constant presence or the fact that she'd been sleeping in my bed.

"You're being discharged," Mason announces, walking into the room, waking up Lauren, who was peacefully snoring only seconds ago.

"Finally, we're going home," I tell a sleepy Lauren, tucking a strand of her hair behind her ear, giving her the good news in case she missed it.

"Great," she says on a yawn while stretching her arms.

*Hospital beds really aren't meant to be slept in.*

Shifting to the edge of the bed, I slide off and turn around before I tell Mason, "We'll be right out. I just need to have a talk with Lauren."

We've been here about twenty-four hours. And I slept most of the time because of the sedation and the exhaustion, unable to talk about what had happened.

As Mason closes the door behind him, Lauren gets up from the bed on the other side before she looks at me. "You want to have a word here?"

I can see the angst in her eyes.

The habit of running away still a reflex.

"We're going to have a word here," I say resolutely.

I refuse to leave this hospital without one. She has to know where I stand before we go back to our lives.

"You would've never let me do it," she confesses, getting straight to the point, while she stays in place even though the door is right behind her.

"Damn straight I wouldn't have," I say as I keep myself from moving toward her, cornering her, as I would normally do.

"I wanted to help."

"By getting yourself killed?" I hiss, having no fucking clue what went on in that head of hers as she planned her whole suicide mission.

She shakes her head, her eyes full of remorse. "No, I never wanted that," she says, eyes fixed on my injured arm.

Probably thinking about the bullet that was meant for her.

The one I wouldn't hesitate to take again.

But the fact that's eating me inside out is that, even now, she's concerned about me and not caring about herself.

"If we hadn't gotten there on time, Frank's accomplice would've killed you." They are harsh words, yet I'm way beyond sugarcoating. I need to make her see.

Fiddling with the blankets, she murmurs, "I know."

"Do you?" I push further, my feet still glued to the floor beneath me. "Because, in that case, you would've left Kate and Sarah behind, completely devastated with a permanent hole in their chests. You would've left Greg and Vance to mourn over your loss for the rest of their lives. You would've given Matthew, Mason, and the whole team a never-ending feeling of failure, grief, and pain. You would've left me"—I swallow down my emotions—"the person who loves you unconditionally." I pause. "More than you love yourself."

She said it only a day ago, confessed her love to me, yet I know it's still a difficult bridge to cross. I know she's afraid of commitment. Our relationship will be something she needs to adjust to, which I don't mind. I just need to know that, when things get rough, when the need to run rises again, she'll run to me.

That's why I disregard every muscle in my body that is straining to make a move in her direction, and remain where I am.

A stretch of silence.

A moment frozen in time.

A chance to choose me.

Or run out the door.

I don't know if I would be able to let her leave if she chose the second option, but I'm happy she's walking toward me.

With shaky hands and wary eyes, she approaches me, doing something that feels as unnatural as me remaining in place.

"I'm sorry," she says as she stands in front of me, tears swimming in her eyes, a small distance in between us.

I can see how she yearns for my touch, aching for my embrace.

Luckily, I have only one arm I need to hold back from reaching out to her.

"I'm so sorry," she repeats as she slowly takes ahold of my hand, initiating first contact.

I've had enough of a restraint session for today—or in this lifetime.

"Come here." I curl my arm around her, pulling her flush against my body, squeezing her to my chest with my right arm as every sob vibrates against my chest.

"I want you to know," I say once she quiets down, lifting her chin, so she looks up to me, "that I can't sleep without you by my side. That I can't breathe without you standing next to me." The thought of her not being here is unbearable. "Don't leave me in the dark. Maybe I wouldn't have agreed with your plan, but I haven't changed my mind. I would do anything for you. That includes stopping the girl I love when she's about to make a huge mistake."

She has no words for me, but the glint in her eyes and the fact that she's in my arms and not out the door are enough of a promise.

She's aced the test, which earns her a kiss.

Then, our eyes lock, and I give her one more vow. "We're in this together."

# Chapter 58
## LAUREN

*Two Weeks Later*

I'm lying on a lounge chair by the pool, my Ray-Bans on, my eyes enthralled with the glistening of the water beneath the midday sun.

That is, until a hard object disrupts my dazed state by landing hard on my flowery bikini top.

"Hey!" I scream, hunting down the owner of the sunscreen that was just thrown my way.

"Sorry, sis," Kate pleads with raised hands. "I thought you saw it coming." She smiles, apologetic. "But I've got *strict* orders from your man," she goes on, pointing in the direction of the terrace.

My eyes flick toward the barbeque where Matthew, Mason, Liam, Dean, and Jaden are bonding over a chunk of meat.

"And what might that *strict* order be?"

"Well, let's just say, you'd better start rubbing that on. Otherwise, he'll do it for ya." She grins, stretching out in the lounge chair on my right side.

She's been having too much fun with our bickering sessions.

"I've already done that," I snap. "This morning, right before I decided to get into my bikini."

"That was like"—she looks at her watch—"seven hours ago."

"My skin is still sticky. I'm not doing it again," I state while I throw the sunscreen on the ground.

"You sure like to push his buttons." Sarah sighs, her head turning my way, as she's on my left side, also sunbathing.

"I'm not gonna argue on that one." I smile as I take a glimpse in his direction, unable to ignore the dark look he's sending my way even though he's in the middle of what seems to be a serious conversation, according to the hand gestures.

As much as I've opened up and tried to listen to him, it still feels unnatural for me to jump at every command, especially when it's about these insignificant details.

Or when I'm right, which is almost always.

"He loves you; be gentle with him," Sarah continues.

While Kate's the one sitting front row, popcorn in hand, enjoying our fights—*she's so Team Liam*—Sarah still has a hard time dealing with our endless discussions.

"I know," I confirm, suppressing the memory of him getting hurt because of me.

It's still a hard pill to swallow. Luckily, the bullet didn't leave any structural or vascular damage, although it had to be surgically removed.

The fact that he couldn't sleep or eat when I ran away cost him much more.

"I didn't expect any different from you," a voice whispers right next to my ear.

As a reflex, I turn to my side, an arm flailing out, as I shriek, "Liam!"

He catches it in the air, his hand sliding toward mine.

"Don't scare me like that!" I yell, still on edge.

"Lauren"—he squeezes my hand—"you're safe here," he vows, a flicker of remorse crossing his eyes before they're set with determination. "Nothing will happen to you."

Even though Daniel Cameron—the guy who shot Liam at the mall—is behind bars, Frank is still out there, free to do what he wants.

The FBI, Vance, SPISe—they're all working together to stop Frank and the whole organization. But like Matthew said, it's complex and still dangerous for me and my sister.

It's the main reason we're on vacation in the middle of nowhere, renting an enormous mansion, enough room for everyone to be here, including Greg, Vance, and Mr. Rabbit. His real name is Brad, but I still call him Mr. Rabbit. They're all here to come up with a plan.

"I know," I say when the weight on my shoulders doesn't go unnoticed.

It's freaky how Liam has always been able to read me, even before I opened up to him.

He pulls me up to stand with him, his arms closing around me when I notice both Sarah and Kate have moved to the terrace, joining the others around the table.

*Traitors.*

Yet I have a smile on my face—one of those that Sarah has a patent on—my heart swelling with joy.

It's been one hell of a year.

Too many times, I felt broken, empty, and alone.

All I want is for this moment to replace all the bad.

All I wish is for this feeling to last forever.

Because this, right here and now—surrounded by people who've come to love and care about me, in the arms of a guy who fits me perfectly by being my opposite—is what I would've missed if I'd kept them away.

I might still have a tendency to build a wall.

But, now, I'm building it around this whole family.

They're all included.

"I love you, too," he says out of the blue when he gives me a kiss on the forehead.

Even though I love Liam with everything I have to give him, I haven't been able to say it back, not since our little moment in the backseat.

"I didn't say anything," I whisper, a little dazzled as I look up at him.

"I've told you before"—his finger brushes along my lips—"I don't need you to say anything. Your body speaks a thousand words."

Tears well in the corners of my eyes.

It's my turn to kiss him.

A mind-blowing, fiercely loving, everlasting kiss.

Proof that this isn't a dream.

That William Drew Ressler is real.

The guy who taught me to run toward people instead of away.

The only guy who deserves to hear me say the words out loud.

"William," I murmur his full name before I finish it off with, "I. Love. You."

Want to read how the story continues from Kate's POV?
Find out in *Save Me*, the second book of the SPISe series.
Turn the page to read a teaser

# Teaser Save Me

"Mason?" I whisper desperately, my phone pressed close to my ear.

"Kate? Where are you?" he yells, worry dripping off every syllable.

I clutch my phone tighter as I can't hold the tears any longer. "Oh God, Mason. I heard a gunshot. They're inside. They're here. They …"

"Kate, breathe."

"I can't." Choking back a sob, I explain, "They have guns, Mase."

"Listen to me, Kate."

"I can't go through this again. I can't be lucky twice," I ramble as more tears make their way down. "They'll find me, and then they'll—"

"Kate, baby, you listen to me now," he demands in such a voice that I press my lips together. "I'm coming for you. Do you hear me?"

I cover my mouth with my hand to smother another sob.

"Kate?" He pauses before he goes on, his voice low yet fierce, "Do you hear me?"

I wipe away my tears with the back of my hand. "I hear you."

"I'm going to save you."

My breath quivers as I inhale his words.

"Kate, say it and believe it."

Looking up, my eyes fixed on the door in front of me, I repeat his words, "You're gonna save me."

"Yes. I. Am."

# Acknowledgments

I have to start by thanking my husband and my kids
for giving me time off to write when I needed it.
And my husband specifically, for believing in me.
For ensuring me that writing is more important than a clean
house.

A special thanks to Randi.
She started off as a beta reader but ended up being so much
more.
A coach, a supporter, a friend.
One who believed from the start that I had the capacity to do
this,
who made me believe in myself.
Every writer deserves to have a Randi.

I also want to thank my beta readers, family, and friends for
their support and enthusiasm. For reading my novel, even
when it wasn't nearly finished.

# Acknowledgments

And, last but definitely not least, my readers.
You.
Who were captivated by the cover or intrigued by the blurb.
Who wanted to read my novel.
Who decided to give a new author a chance.
**Thank you!**
I hope you loved it.
And I hope you'll be back for more.
Much love,

*Julia*

PS: I would be so grateful
if you could leave a review for CATCH ME
on Amazon, Goodreads
or whichever site you purchased from.
Even if it's only one sentence, it would still be awesome!

# About The Author

Julia Crosswood is a teacher and a mom of two by day.
A writer and avid reader by night—or when
the kids are napping.
Although writing and self-publishing her books
take a lot of time, she makes sure there's enough left
to make sweet memories with her family,
including lots of vacations—yet it's never
without her laptop or Kindle.

# About The Author

Visit her website at www.juliacrosswood.com
Follow her on Twitter: https://twitter.com/JuliaCrosswood
Follow her on Instagram:
https://www.instagram.com/juliacrosswood
Don't forget to sign up for Julia's newsletter on her website.

www.ingramcontent.com/pod-product-compliance
Lightning Source LLC
Chambersburg PA
CBHW070341010826

48976CB00017B/699